Every Little Thing

Every Little Thing

Published by Babel Press U.S.A.

This book was originally published in Japanese under the title
"エブリ リトル シング"
by Kodansha Ltd., Tokyo, Japan in 2010.

Author: Ash Omurah

Director: Tomoki Hotta

Translator: Zal Heiwa Sethna
Coordinator: Junko Rodriguez
Formatting: Sota Torigoe

ISBN: 978-0989232609

Babel Corporation
Pacific Business News Bldg. #208,
1833 Kalakaua Avenue,
Honolulu, Hawaii 96815

Phone: (808) 946 - 3773
Fax: (808) 946 - 3993

Website: http://www.bookandright.com/

Table of Contents

Every Little Thing

The Boy and the Beetles

At an insect shop located in a department store, a young boy stared intently at stag beetles in a cage located deep inside the store. Nearby, the shopkeeper stacked insect food on a shelf.

The young boy turned to the shopkeeper. "Hey, Mister!"

"Hey there, little guy," the shopkeeper replied, a canister of insect food still in his hand. "Do you want to buy a stag beetle?"

"Yeah, but I kinda had a question. How do you decide how much a stag beetle costs?"

"You mean the price?"

"Yeah, the price."

"Well, it mostly comes down to the beetle's size and the shape of its mandibles. The bigger it is and the better its mandibles look, the more expensive it is."

The boy stared back at the shopkeeper, puzzled. "Really? That's weird."

"Why's that?"

"Well," the boy began to explain. "The stag beetles in those cages over there all cost ¥3,000, right? So, how come these ones are so cheap?" The boy pointed at the "¥300" sign taped to the cage in front of him. "I mean, they look pretty big and their mandibles look really cool. And there are only two of these guys, but a whole bunch of the others. Is everyone buying them because they're so cheap? Is that why there are only two?"

Here we go again, the shopkeeper thought. He sighed, looking down at the boy. "Not really. Take a good look at these two beetles, little guy. They've only got five legs."

"*Five*?"

The boy squinted into the cage and began counting the beetles' legs. "One, two, three, four... five. You're right, it's got five legs. And this one has: one, two, three, four, five. It's also got five legs!"

The boy took this in and fell silent.

"Yeah, too bad right? They're both missing a leg. Sometimes the trappers get a little rough with the beetles, and they end up losing a leg."

The boy remained silent, just staring at the beetles, engrossed. The shopkeeper, relieved at having unloaded this unpleasant secret, jovially chatted away.

"Just bad luck, you know? Anyway, they're just taking up space now, seeing as no one wants a stag beetle with a missing leg. They've been here since yesterday and nobody's bought them—not even at this price."

The boy stood still, biting his lip. The shop was so quiet, that they could hear the fibrous fluttering of the beetles' wings.

Finally, the boy spoke again.

"Okay, I've decided. I'm going to buy this stag beetle."

"This one? The one with a missing leg?"

"It still has five."

The boy's determination caught the shopkeeper off guard. He felt a twinge of doubt. "Well, if that's what you want, I'm not going to stop you. But let me ask you this—is it because you don't have enough money?

"Nope. I've got ¥5,000 on me."

The shopkeeper laughed, relieved. "Well, then don't bother with these guys. Go ahead and get yourself a normal beetle."

"A normal beetle?"

"Yeah. Come on, I'll show you. I'll tell you all about the different kinds of stag beetles we've got.
And, you know, if you still want to buy one of these defective guys, I'll throw one in for free! Nobody's going to buy them, anyway."

The shopkeeper grabbed the boy's hand and began toward the ¥3,000 beetles. The boy remained staring at the five-legged beetles. "W-wait, Mister!" the boy cried, but the shopkeeper kept walking and knocked the boy off of his balance and he fell to the floor...

CLANG! A metallic clamor echoed through the store.

"What was that?" The shopkeeper quickly glanced around the room, but there was nobody in the store but him and the boy. Relieved, the shopkeeper apologized to the boy.
"Hey, I'm sorry about that. Are you okay?

The boy nodded.

"Oh good! Um... did you notice... was it just me, or did you hear something just now? Like a metal bat dropping to the floor?"

The boy stood and, hesitant, rolled up the right leg of his trousers. "It's just this," the boy replied.

The shopkeeper's eyes widened as he realized what had caused the clamor. "That's a…"

"Yeah. It's a prosthetic leg. But it's made to look exactly like my skin color, so it's kinda hard to tell."

"A prosthetic leg?" he tried not to stammer.

"I lost my right leg when I was in second grade. I've been using a prosthetic leg ever since."

The shopkeeper, dumbfounded, searched for the right words, but there were none.

"You know what?" the boy said. "I know I'm missing my right leg, but I've never thought of myself as not normal or defective. I mean, I can't run around like my friends or play soccer like I want to… but I can still walk to school."

"Is that right?" the shopkeeper finally spoke. "So, um, how far do you walk to get to school?"

"About half a mile. Oh, and remember how you were telling me that nobody wants a stag beetle missing a leg? Well, I've got lots of friends at school, and they even voted me class president. And… hey, mister? Are you listening?"

The shopkeeper had become lost in his thoughts. "Yeah, yeah. Sure, I'm listening. So, you're class president, huh? That's pretty impressive."

"Yeah! And look. I've only got one of my two legs left, but these stag beetles have five of their six legs left. Mathematically, they have more legs than I do. If I had six legs, I'd only have three left." The boy smiled, proud.

"I remember learning that stuff in school when I was your age. So, you like math, huh?

"Yeah! I'm going to grow up and win the Nobel Prize in math!"

"Nobel Prize, huh? That's a pretty big dream you've got there."

"Anyway, these beetles are so much bigger and have way cooler mandibles than those ¥3,000 beetles. That's why I want to get one!"

The boy's enthusiasm put the shopkeeper at ease. Now, he found himself trying to compete with the boy's gusto.

"You got it, little guy! One five-legged beetle coming right up!"

"Thanks, mister!"

"Or... what do you say? Want to take both of these guys home?"

"Um...." The boy considered this for a moment. "I'll just take one."

The shopkeeper skillfully scooped the five-legged stag beetle into a thin cardboard box, and handed it over to the boy along with his change of ¥4,700. Then, he noticed the canister of insect food he'd been holding in his hand the entire time.

"I'll tell you what. You can have this insect food, too."

"You mean for free?"

"Absolutely."

"Wow, thanks! But are you sure? It says ¥700. It's even more expensive than the beetle!

"Don't worry about it. Think of it as a little gift for teaching me a very important lesson."

"You mean about math?"

"Math?" The shopkeeper laughed warmly. "Yeah, something like that."

The shopkeeper smiled sheepishly, waving goodbye as he watched the boy walk away with the newly purchased five-legged stag beetle. Every other step produced a dull metallic clang.

Once the boy was out of sight, the shopkeeper walked over to the cage containing the remaining five-legged beetle and added a zero at the end of the 300.

The Lunchbox

1

"The area where we take off our shoes is, like, sooo huge. Dad says that's why he went for a Western-style front door that swings inwards instead of the usual ones that swing outwards. It doesn't get in the way even if someone's putting on their shoes inside, you know? So what about your house, Lisa? Does your door swing inwards or outwards?"

Lisa was so consumed with suppressing the panic in her stomach that she couldn't reply.

It was spring and Lisa was visiting Imari's home for the first time since becoming close friends, by the simple luck of sitting next to each other in class.

By summertime, Lisa had become a fixture at Imari's house. With Lisa at her side, Imari pushed open her hefty front door and bounded inside. As usual, she announced her arrival.

"I'm home! God, I'm starving."

Imari's mother appeared in the hallway. She was a lovely woman who moved with such elegance that her slippers didn't make a sound.

"Hello, Lisa, how are you?" Imari's mother said, then turned to Imari." Imari, there's no need to announce your hunger the second you arrive. It's childish. Isn't that right, Lisa?"

Although her words were scolding, Imari's mother's eyes were warm as she smiled at Lisa.

"Hi, Mrs. Zaitsu," Lisa replied, bowing her head.

Behind Imari's mother stretched a lengthy red-carpeted hallway. It was decorated with what Lisa assumed were expensive works of art—although she wouldn't know for sure—precisely adorning the walls. Hanging from the ceiling was a chandelier. Lisa thought about her classmate, Gaku, who had mispronounced it "Cinderella" in English class and had yet to live it down.

I bet they could fit a whole other room in here if they wanted, Lisa thought, gawking at the ceiling.

While Lisa's gaze remained upward, Imari kicked off her shoes. "Where's Dad?" she asked.

"He's home. It'll be the four of us for dinner again. Come in, Lisa."

Imari's mother laid out a pair of fluffy slippers for Lisa, giving a hospitable smile.

"Thanks, Mrs. Zaitsu," she replied, but her voice was soon lost underneath the clomping of Imari's slippers as she stomped her way to the kitchen.

"Imari," her mother said. "No thumping."

Lisa's eyes met with Imari's mother and they shared a soft, knowing laugh. When Imari's mother looked away, Lisa sighed.

Imari's dad is always home at this time. And these slippers her mom always lays out for me—I bet I could buy a new dress for the kind of money they probably cost. What does her dad do, anyway? How can he afford such an amazing house?

Every day after cram school, Lisa would drop by Imari's house and was often invited to stay for dinner—a proposal that she always eagerly accepted. Dinner was served in a combined kitchen-dining room which had a TV all its own, even though there was one in the living room. Imari's kitchen TV was far bigger than the only TV in Lisa's home, but ever since Lisa had been staying for dinner, it had disappeared into the background.

"I've got to tell you, Lisa," Imari's father said, "ever since you've been joining us for dinner, I feel like I have two daughters. It feels great."

While pouring wine for her husband, Imari's mother winked at Lisa. She knew what was coming.

"Fine," Imari said, "I guess one wasn't good enough for you." Then she stuck her tongue out at her father. The four of them laughed, their reflections blurring in the dark rectangle of the TV screen. If the TV had ears, it would come to the conclusion, from this ebullient chatter, that it had been rendered irrelevant—that the family no longer had any use for it. Although the thing was only taking up space now, there were plenty of people who would love to have a TV this big in their living room—present company included.

"Let's go up to my room," Imari said to Lisa as she finished the last of her food.

"Give me your lunchbox first, Imari," her mother reminded her as they were about to leave the room. "I need to wash it with the dishes. I don't see why I have to remind you everyday."

"Oh, yeah, right." As Imari dug around in her school bag, Lisa stared at the large dishwasher in the kitchen.

"Here," Imari said handing her lunchbox off to her mother, who took the lunchbox and placed it in the dishwasher.

"Thank you for dinner, Mrs. Zaitsu," Lisa politely said.

"You're very welcome, Lisa."

The dishwasher began to hum quietly.

In her room, Imari tossed her schoolbag onto her bed— a king-sized affair, large enough for both Imari and Lisa to lie comfortably side-by-side. And this extravagance did not stop at the bed. The desk was long enough for both of them to sit and work (with plenty of room to spare) and Imari's *two* wardrobes were grander and of a higher quality than any Lisa had ever seen in any of the outlet stores where she had been.

"By the way," Imari said, flippant, opening one of the wardrobes and pulling out a long dress. "I'm not going to wear this anymore. Do you want it?"

Lisa kept her gaze locked on the dress—a response ready to dart out. It found its way to her throat then stuck there—a jagged, stinging lump. She conjured up a courteous response instead.

"Are you going to throw it away?"

"Um. I mean, if you don't want it, I'll probably just throw it out. So...? Do you want it?"

Lisa's eyes shifted from the outfit to the floor. She softly shook her head.

2

"See you tomorrow, Imari!"

Lisa left the Zaitsu residence and headed home. When she arrived, she unlocked the front door and, with difficulty, dragged it open along its uneven threshold.

I wish doors were either pushed or pulled open. I'll bet Imari has never seen a door like this outside of school.

Lisa sighed and headed to her room. A few steps down her hallway, which was painted with an unusual garish glossiness, Lisa slid open a door (which was slotted over an even more difficult threshold) and entered her small bedroom with its tattered tatami mats, a squat desk she'd had since she was six, and a comparatively miniscule wardrobe. Her futon was neatly folded away in the built-in closet.

Lisa took off her school uniform and put on something comfortable. She removed her pink cloth-wrapped lunchbox from her schoolbag and headed to the small kitchen, which was located only a few steps away from the front door. She turned on the water faucet, added a dab of detergent and carefully cleaned her lunchbox. When she was finished, she dried it off with a dishtowel.

It was already nine o'clock on a weekday, but there was still plenty left for Lisa to do. She returned to her room, rolled her shoulders a couple of times to re-energize herself, and then sat down at her desk, opening her notebook and textbook. Once three hours had passed, she decided she'd done enough for the day and that is was high time for a bath. She sat and soaked for an extended period of time—enough pampering to address the skincare needs of a 15-year-old at the threshold of womanhood. By the time Lisa got out of the bath and put on her pajamas, it was one in the morning.

Any minute now.

The second that the thought popped into her mind, she detected her father's presence at the front door. It was not that she had a gift for foresight—it was that her father was precise and predicable with his 1:00 a.m. return from work.

As the front door skidded and dragged shut, Lisa grabbed a cold can of beer from the fridge.

"I'm home!" her father called. He headed straight for the dining room and collapsed into a chair without bothering to change out of his work clothes. The chair whined under the force of his weight—he was not a small man.

Psssht! Lisa opened the can and handed it to her father.

"Here you go, Dad."

"Oh, hey. Thanks!"

Her father took the can in his calloused right hand and began chugging, his Adam's apple bobbing up and down as he swallowed.

"Aaah. I tell you, Lisa, beer is mankind's greatest invention.

If I could go back in time, I'd give a Nobel Prize to the guy who invented beer."

Lisa couldn't help but smile at her father's tired but endearing beer philosophy. And she knew what was coming next.

"It's already past one, Lisa. I know you're trying to help around the house as much as you can, but you really need your rest."

Despite these protests, every night Lisa's father would enjoy listening to his daughter talk excitedly about her day. He could feel himself slacken in the peacefulness that this precious time with his daughter always brought him.

Lisa, however, never talked about Imari.

Once Lisa finished with her stories of the day, her father walked over to the fridge to retrieve his second beer of the night. "Well, I'm going to bed," Lisa said. "Don't stay up too late."

"Don't worry," her father replied and toasted his beer in the air. "Once I'm done with this one, I'll take a bath and hit the hay. You know, sometimes I wish we had a shower so it wouldn't take so long to clean up."

"I don't know why you hate soaking in the bath so much. If I had a Nobel Prize to give away, I'd totally give it to the guy who invented the bathtub."

Lisa's father smiled—his daughter was growing up so quickly.

This was a typical day in the life of Lisa.

It was the last summer of junior high. Lisa was busy studying for the entrance exams she'd have to pass in six months to be accepted to La Versa Academy—the most prestigious local private high school. During the day she went to summer school followed by cram school at night. After cram school, she would return home to hours of studying.

The mornings were always a fierce battle with drowsiness—the potential for even an extra minute of rest threatening to swallow her back into sleep. Still, somehow, she found the time to sit in front of the mirror in her school uniform and meticulously do her hair. This had become the most essential phase of her morning ritual, even if it meant skipping breakfast.

Perfect, she thought to herself as she got up to leave, moving quietly, hoping not to wake her father. The silence, of course, was obliterated by the grinding cacophony of the front door. Still, neither her silence nor the door mattered—to this day, not once had the door's clamor yanked her father from his deep slumber.

3

Dai laid down his chopsticks as he finished his breakfast. He looked up at his wife with a wide, happy smile. In return, Ayu handed him a lunchbox wrapped in a blue cloth.

"Here, Dai."

"Thanks! Hmm… is there a frankfurter octopus in there? Does it have two legs or four?"

Ayu didn't reply.

"Seriously, though, aren't you getting sick of making my lunch every day? I bet you can't wait for fall term to start so I can go back to school lunches."

"To be honest—sure, it's much easier for me when you're eating school lunches. But, you know, this is only for the summer."

"Well, I'd rather be eating homemade lunches. That way, every once in a while, I know I'll open my lunchbox and find my rice decorated with seasoning in the shape of a heart."

"Don't be silly, Dai. You're not going to get a frankfurter octopus, nor are you getting hearts on your rice. You're not a kid anymore. Soon, you're going to be a dad."

Ayu rubbed her stomach and Dai eagerly leaned his ear into it.

"What're you doing?"

"Trying to hear what Yuko's saying."

"Yuko? We don't even know if it's a boy or a girl yet. Anyway, you need to be going. It doesn't look good for the teacher to come in late, especially when those kids are skipping their summer break to come to class."

"Yeah, yeah."

"One yeah, Dai."

Ayu would be going on maternity leave at the end of the summer and a year of childcare leave after that. She had already begun to slip into the role of the no-nonsense mom and found herself taking a scolding tone in correcting her husband's behavior.

And Dai found himself already acting as though he were a dad.

Ayu and Dai stood at the front door saying good-bye.

"So you get maternity leave *and* childcare leave? Lucky you."

"Lucky? Want to trade places?"

Dai smiled uneasily, images of painful birth scenes from TV popping into his mind. He shook his head, kissed his wife goodbye, and left for work.

This was an ordinary day in the simple, happy life of Dai.

4

On a normal school day, the students of Minami-sakura Middle School would eat their school lunches in designated groups; but it was now summer vacation, and the students came in carrying lunches lovingly prepared by their parents, eating them however and wherever they felt like—whether it was a solitary student eating with an open textbook in one hand, a boy and girl enjoying each other's company, or a chatty group of six.

That day, Dai decided to not eat alone at his desk as he normally did. Instead, he decided to join a couple of girl students who ate in the classroom and always seemed to have fun together.

They were spending their precious summer vacation coming into class—the least he could do was demonstrate that he cared.

He pulled up an empty desk. "Hey, Lisa. Imari. Mind if I join you girls?"

"Not at all, Mr. Watanabe!" Imari replied brightly. Lisa, on the other hand, clearly was not too keen on the idea, and Dai failed to notice until he was already sitting down.

Hmm, Dai thought. *Did I do something to upset Lisa? Or... I get it. She's sitting here, having a great time with her friend, and I just butted in. I should have thought this through more carefully.*

But now he had already pulled up a desk and gained Imari's enthusiastic approval. It would be awkward to defer to Lisa and back out. Though he felt bad for Lisa, he felt the best course of action was to stay.

Overcompensating for his awkward feelings, Dai pulled out his lunchbox with dramatic flair, unwrapping the blue cloth that covered it.

"So, Mr. Watanabe… I have a question. Is it true you can tell a man is in a loving marriage if his lunch comes with a frankfurter octopus or seasoning in the shape of a heart?"

"Don't be silly, Imari," he replied quickly. "Once you become an adult you stop indulging in that kind of nonsensical cuteness."

Imari's teasing seemed to help Lisa loosen up a bit.

Thank god for Imari. She sure knows how to break the ice, Dai thought, and he was able to relax a little as well. He sighed with relief and opened his lunchbox. Immediately, he tensed up again. There in his lunchbox was a frankfurter octopus, its tail end cut into four curling legs. The rice, meanwhile, featured a patch of seasoning sprinkled perfectly in the shape of a heart.

Embarrassed, he slammed the lid shut, flipped the lunchbox over, and opened the bottom lid instead. It was a rush decision, an improvisation—a desperate attempt to make the bottom look like the top so the girls would not see the heart shape laid out lovingly over the white rice. All he had to figure out now was a way to surreptitiously eat the frankfurter octopus before they could see it… but it was too late. Imari had gotten a good look at his lunch the second he opened the top lid.

"Oh my god! You have both! A frankfurter octopus *and* a heart on your rice! Did you come to join us so you could show off, Mr. Watanabe?!"

Imari felt so bold and proud of how prescient she had been that she snatched the lunchbox away from Dai, who was now cripplingly flustered.

"H-hey Imari, give it back!" he warned, but his words failed at having any authority. Imari flipped the lunchbox once and threw open the top lid.

"Hmm. A four-legged frankfurter octopus!"

"Okay, that's enough." Dai struggled to hide his embarrassment. He scratched his head in an attempt to disguise it. *Geez, Ayu! Of all the days for you to put in a frankfurter octopus and a heart design on the rice!*

"Hey, Lisa?" Imari said cheerfully. "Did it just suddenly get hot in here?"

"What?"

"Oh, wait, it's just the love burning up in this lunchbox!" Imari laughed and raised the lunchbox into the air. Her voice rang around the classroom. Other students began to notice and gathered around.

"No way! An octopus!"

"Yeah, I remember those. I used get them in my lunchbox too…when I was in preschool!"

"Is that a heart on top of your rice, Mr. Watanabe?"

"Dude, you know what that means. Mr. and Mrs. Watanabe are still hot for each other!"

There was no longer any use for Dai to lie about the contents of his lunchbox, so he scrambled. "Come on, guys. You've got it all wrong. My wife is having a kid soon, so she's just doing this for practice."

The fib only enflamed the students' enthusiasm.

"Oh my god! Your wife's pregnant?!"

"Um, yeah. Eight months."

"Eight months!" exclaimed one student, Gaku. "What're you doing coming to school, Mr. Watanabe?! Come to think of it, how *do* you make kids?"

Imari jabbed Gaku in the head for asking such a blunt question. His lack of knowledge apparently wasn't limited to his mispronunciation of English words.

"Ow! What? This is more important than math, Imari!"

"You are such a pervert!"

"Hey, I want to know too," another student, Takashi, added. "Even after all that stuff about stamens and pistils, I still don't get it!" Takashi was also a bit of a dim bulb. Seeing as he didn't understand plant reproduction, an explanation of human intercourse would probably make his brain explode.

Oh well, Dai thought with a smile. *Can't blame them for asking these questions at this age.*

Hoping that Imari would calm things down eventually, Dai casually glanced at Imari and Lisa's lunchboxes. Neither girl had even finished half their lunch. Then, examining the two lunchboxes, something struck him as being odd.

When given a photograph showing a set of traffic lights with the order of the lights reversed, only a few viewers would be able to immediately identify the mistake—but many would still notice that something was off. This is how Dai felt about the lunchboxes.

He closed his eyes and tried to figure out what was out of place. He gave up and opened his eyes. Lisa was putting the lid back on her lunchbox.

"You're not eating anymore, Lisa? Are you all right?"

"Oh, yeah, um, my stomach's feeling a little funny."

"Will you be all right for the afternoon?"

"Yeah, of course," Lisa replied as she wrapped her lunchbox in a pink cloth.

Meanwhile, Imari had managed to put both Gaku and Takashi in a headlock under each of her arms.

"Come on, Imari, finish up. Lunchtime's almost over. The rest of you, go back to your seats."

Once everyone had returned to their seats, Dai took his lunchbox back from Imari. He flipped it over to eat his lunch from the less conspicuous side. But, realizing that all of the students now knew about the cute touches his wife had applied to his lunch, he decided there was no longer any point in hiding it. He flipped the lunchbox back to its original side and opened the top lid, revealing the heart-decorated rice in all its glory.

Right at that moment, it clicked into place—Dai figured out what it was that had been nagging at him.

I hope I'm wrong. But if I'm right, it all makes sense.

Later that day, the students were attentively listening to Dai as he conducted the afternoon class. It was a marked difference from the commotion that had taken place in the classroom during lunch. The topic was absolute conditions. The students diligently took notes, asking questions until they were sure they understood the material.

The seriousness of his students as they earnestly soaked up all the information inspired Dai to give them everything they needed and more.

These kids have their whole lives ahead of them. If there's anything I can do to help them grow, it's my duty to do it.

5

The next morning, Dai woke up early to make a phone call.

"Hey, Dai...?"Ayu spoke as he put down the receiver.

"I just spoke to Bando. He wasn't sure last night, but now he says he can cover periods one and two for me."

"That's great. Anyway...I know you said I didn't need to make lunch for you today, but..." Ayu trailed off as she searched his eyes.

"Not just today, Ayu. You don't have to make me lunch for the rest of the summer."

"It's not a big deal, actually, you know? I kinda like it."

Dai smiled to himself, remembering the frankfurter octopus and heart-on-rice. "Don't worry about it. I'm just trying a little... experiment. Trust me."

She continued to search his eyes. Dai laid a reassuring hand on her shoulder.

Dai left the house half an hour earlier than usual and stopped at a nearby convenience store. Afterwards, he didn't head for school, but headed somewhere else completely.

As soon as he arrived at his destination, he stopped and took the time to soak in his surroundings. Around ten minutes later, he began walking again. This was only his second time walking down this street—the first time was a home visitation in May.

After a while, Dai caught sight of a convenience store. He

stopped for a few minutes in front of the store, but then continued on his way.

About 200 yards further down the road, he came upon an alleyway on his right. He turned into the alleyway and stopped there, turning to peek out from around the corner. He lingered there for a while in hopes that his hypothesis was simply the result of an overactive imagination. However, those hopes were soon quashed as the very scenario he had expected began to play out in front of his eyes.

A sharp pain ran through his heart; he bit down on his lip. After a moment of panged vacillation, Dai stepped out from the alleyway.

"Hi, Lisa."

Lisa, crouched on the ground, looked up and stared straight into Dai's concerned eyes. "Mr. Watanabe!" she blurted out, quickly hiding her hands behind her back as she scrambled to stand up. The pink cloth that had been resting on her knees fluttered to the ground.

"What… what are you doing here?" Lisa's cheeks had turned bright red, and her large, unblinking black eyes looked like the round, glass eyes of a doll. She stood frozen in place, shaking very slightly.

"I'm really sorry, Lisa. I didn't mean to scare you like that." Dai had not expected Lisa to react with such shock, and he now found himself in an awkward position. The two were never supposed to meet in this place and at this time. With no one else around to break the tension, they stood silently in place. Finally, Lisa spoke.

"Did you follow me here, Mr. Watanabe? That's really not cool." She tried to steady her knees and the hands she hid behind her back, but to no avail. Giving up, Lisa looked away from Dai and stared into empty space. Then her eyes lowered and, one by one, tears began to drop and collect onto the cloth that lay on the ground.

"I'm really sorry, Lisa. I didn't want to hurt your feelings. I just wanted to talk with you."

The wet patch on the cloth continued to grow.

"Hey, Lisa? Why don't you skip class for the morning? I'll skip class with you. You want to go get coffee somewhere?"

Surprised by her teacher's encouragement of truancy, Lisa blinked and looked up. Dai stared back with steady compassionate eyes. Lisa found herself nodding. She noticed she had regained feeling in her knees.

"Great. But before that, why don't you put whatever you're holding in your hands down on the ground? You can't dry your eyes if your hands are full." Dai offered her a handkerchief.

Lisa revealed what she had been clutching the whole time—her empty lunchbox in her left hand, and a ready-made meal in her right.

6

By the time they arrived at the coffee shop, Lisa's eyes had dried. Dai sent Lisa to grab a table in the back of the shop while he ordered two iced coffees. When he arrived at the table, he carried a tray with the coffees, one plastic carton of cream, and another of simple syrup.

"Here you go. I'm guessing you're not yet ready for black coffee, so I brought these." Dai added the cream and syrup to Lisa's coffee and stirred until it was all mixed together. Lisa observed the process curiously, having never visited a coffee shop in her life. Dai handed the coffee to Lisa.

"Thanks, Mr. Watanabe. You don't take milk or syrup?"

"I'm an adult, Lisa. Of course I drink my coffee black."

Lisa found Dai's defensiveness funny. She tried to hide her amusement, but her face broke into a teasing, dimpled grin. "I don't know, Mr. Watanabe. I still remember that frankfurter octopus and that heart on your rice from yesterday."

Then she took a sip of the coffee. "Mmm. I love it! I never get to drink coffee like this."

Her pure delight put Dai at ease. *That's the Lisa I know.*

"Can I ask you a question, Mr. Watanabe?" Lisa asked. "How did you know? About me putting ready-made meals into my lunchbox?"

"Remember the lunch you had yesterday?"

"Yeah?"

"While I was flipping my lunchbox to hide the heart my wife laid out on top of my rice… before realizing there really wasn't any point after what happened… it occurred to me—wouldn't you normally put the rice in the lunchbox first and *then* place a sheet of *nori* on top?"

"Oh!" Lisa gasped, realizing what had tipped him off.

"Yup. The lunch you brought in had the rice laid out on top of the *nori*. Normally, you wouldn't expect anyone to prepare the rice portion of your lunch like that. But if you already had a meal prepared the right way, and then emptied it out into your lunchbox, the *nori* would come on the bottom."

Lisa listened without saying a word.

"So I thought, why would Lisa have to do that in the first place? That's when I figured it had to have been a ready-made meal you bought at a convenience store."

Lisa turned red as an apple and lowered her lonely gaze to the table.

Dai hurriedly changed tactics. "I'd be a pretty good detective, don't you think?"

Lisa looked up at him again, attempting a happy face. "Yeah. You're like CSI."

7

"When did your mother pass away, Lisa?"

"When I was in sixth grade."

"Just three years ago. Do you still think about her a lot?"

Lisa stirred her coffee with her straw for a moment before replying. "Of course I do. I know she wasn't going to make it through that year, but I still feel like that bus accident took her away from me before I really had a chance to say goodbye. But to be honest, I don't think about her as much as I used to."

"Do you feel like you've come to terms with her death?"

"I think so. But I think it's mostly because I'm worried about my dad. I mean, he comes home from work late every night, and I'm sure it's not the easiest job in the world. He's still fit as an ox, but still."

Dai remembered the big man he met when he went to her home for a visitation.

"But your dad works in a department store, right? Doesn't his shop close when the store closes? Or is there something more to his job?"

Reticent, Lisa pressed her lips together—she was uncomfortable with this topic. "Running an insect shop doesn't really make a lot of money. And even then, he'll give away food and stuff for free, because 'there's nothing like seeing a little kid smile.' He's just not a very good businessman. I don't think he should be running a business in the first place."

Dai sensed she was embarrassed about her father's line of work. "But I can understand that. To me, it just shows how much your dad really cares about his shop and his customers. I really admire him for that."

Lisa brightened up. The thought of someone she admired as much as her teacher expressing admiration toward her father helped her to see her father in a new light. She felt proud, and the elation considerably loosened her up.

"But he doesn't make any money at all from the insect shop, so every day after he work, he goes to another job."

"What does he do?"

"I don't really know. All I know is he comes home every night looking dirty and wearing workman's clothes. So it's probably some kind of manual labor." Lisa sucked up a tiny bit of coffee through the straw, and let its bittersweet flavor linger on her tongue for just a moment. She then began to talk about the time her mother found out her condition was terminal.

"Do you know what my mom said?"

Until you've graduated from middle school, make sure that school is your top priority. There'll be plenty of time to learn to cook in high school. Don't worry about your father; he'll be fine. He once ate dog food and claimed it was delicious. He'll eat anything you cook for him.

"Isn't that horrible?" Lisa said as she puffed her cheeks.

Dai laughed. "She compared your cooking to dog food? So I'm guessing your mother handed over her cooking duties to you. And, with no school lunches over the summer, you've been emptying out ready-made meals into your lunchbox and hoping no one would notice."

There was still something Dai hadn't figured out, and he thought now was the time to ask.

"Where do you get your lunch money from?"

"My dad," Lisa said softly. "He gave me ¥20,000 to spend for lunch this month, and that's in addition to my allowance."

"I see. Well, Lisa, that makes your dad a pretty wonderful guy, wouldn't you say? I'm liking him more and more by the minute."

"Really?"

"Of course," he assured her as he sucked on his straw. But there was only air. He looked down and saw that both his and Lisa's glasses were empty. "What do you say to another coffee?"

"Um, shouldn't we be going back to class?"

"No worries. We'll be back in time for third period."

8

Dai returned to the table with two more iced coffees. Once again, he poured cream and syrup for Lisa and stirred the mixture before handing it over to her. Without a word, Lisa grabbed it and began drinking.

"You know what I think, Lisa? I think that every one of us is living with some kind of handicap. But what's important is not to hide that handicap, but to live as fulfilling a life as you can while living openly with that handicap."

"I still wish I had both parents. And that we were well off."

"There's plenty of money to go around, Lisa. I mean, if it's money you want to make, you can make as much as you want once you've grown up. But can you really be happy with something you're given without having to do any work?"

"What do you mean?"

"Take that iced coffee you're drinking right now as an example. It contains just the right amount of cream and syrup, and you're drinking away at it like it was the most natural thing in the world, but somebody went through the effort to mix in that cream and syrup."

Lisa immediately removed the straw from her mouth.

"Oh, god, I'm so sorry. I forgot to thank you for..."

"Don't worry about it. The point is, when you're given something on a silver platter, you start to expect it all the time. Maybe at some point you stop feeling grateful for anything. Lisa, you've decided to spend your summer holidays attending summer school so you can conquer your weakness in math, in spite of all your difficulties at home. If all this effort pays off, and you get into La Versa, you'll have something to cherish for life."

Dai's words reverberated inside Lisa's mind. At that moment, a vivid memory began to play in her mind—of her scoring a 100 on an English test in her first term of junior high. She had been so proud of the result that she had dashed into the teacher's office to show off to Dai, who was her homeroom teacher that year. She could remember that moment like it happened yesterday. In fact, she was pretty sure she would never forget that particular joy for the rest of her life. It was that moment when she decided she wanted to go to America for college.

"I guess what I want to say is," Dai continued, "so what if you're eating ready-made meals? It's nothing to be embarrassed about. Those meals, Lisa, are paid for by the hard-earned money your dad makes by working late into the night. You should think yourself lucky to have such a great dad. What would he say if he found out about the lunchbox? What would your mom say?"

Lisa considered this.

"Besides, if your biggest handicap is not looking perfect in the eyes of others, you're actually doing all right."

That reminded Lisa of a story her father told her the night before, which she recounted for Dai.

"So that boy ended up buying the five-legged stag beetle?"

"Yeah. And then my dad told me, 'Once you've accepted your handicap, it just becomes a part of your character. And that boy's character shined brighter than anyone I've met in a long time.'"

Dai sipped the last of his coffee and became distracted, remembering something that his wife had told him once.

Didn't Ayu say the class president in her class had only one leg?

9

"Hey, Lisa. Want to see something neat?"

"Um, okay." Lisa stared at him with adorable curiosity as he pulled out a small piece of paper from the inner pocket of his jacket. There was writing on the front, but Dai flipped it over to the other side and began drawing a black circle with a pen.

"All right, Lisa. What do you think this is?"

"Um. A black circle?"

"Bingo. Now, here's my next question. Why is there a black circle on this piece of paper?" Dai was clearly enjoying this as he watched Lisa, perplexed over the black circle.

"Um. Because you drew it there?"

Is this some kind of psychological test?

"Okay, let me try rephrasing the question. Do you think you can erase this black circle?"

"Nope," she replied right away.

"No?" Dai smiled. "Then watch this." Dai began to fill the white areas around the circle with his pen. Soon, the entire piece of paper had turned black, making it impossible to discern anything resembling a shape, let alone a circle.

"See? No more black circle!"

Oookay. So is it a test, or did he just want to show me a magic trick? Lisa rested her head on her hands as she tried to decipher what Dai was getting at. Unfazed by Lisa's confused expression, Dai pulled out another piece of paper and once again drew a black circle on the back.

"I'm going to ask you again, Lisa. Why is there a black circle on this piece of paper?"

Lisa looked back and forth between the now black piece of paper and the white piece of paper with the black circle in the middle. A spark of realization appeared in her eyes—but she could not articulate her thoughts.

"The reason there's a black circle on this piece of paper is because the area around it isn't black. If the surrounding area were black, this black circle would cease to exist. In other words, the absolute condition for a black circle to exist is for it to be in contact with something that isn't black."

The words "absolute condition" took Lisa back to the previous day's math lesson. Dai sensed this was what was going through her mind, and tried to steer her back to the topic at hand.

"It's not math time yet, Lisa."

Lisa quietly stared at the black circle.

Do you understand now, Lisa? No two people are alike in this world. No two lives are the same. That's what makes life interesting. If there are rich people, there will be poor people. But being poor means you'll feel that much more joy when you finally do become rich. In the same way, it's only because you have trouble with math that when you do manage to solve a problem, you feel such unadulterated joy. Today's problems are nothing but temporary debts you've made for the happiness you'll earn in the future. Since these debts never increase over time, all you need to do to pay them back is to achieve the goals you've set for yourself.

But Lisa still gazed at the black circle. Maybe it was a bit too philosophical for a 15-year-old girl.

"You know what, Lisa, forget about it. I was just being goofy." As Dai was about to crumple up both pieces of paper, feeling a bit silly about his over-eagerness, Lisa stopped him.

"Mr. Watanabe? Could I have the one with the black circle on it?"

"This one? Sure, if you want it." Dai handed the piece of paper to Lisa.

"You know what, Mr. Watanabe? I am going to treasure this piece of paper for the rest of my life. Whatever happens, I will always remember this day."

"I think you're going a bit overboard there. We're just having coffee, Lisa." Dai scratched his forehead and looked around the room to mask his embarrassment. Then he saw the clock.

"Uh-oh. We'd better get back to school."

"Okay!" As they got up to leave, Lisa carefully placed the piece of paper in her skirt pocket.

10

"Hope you don't mind, Imari," Dai said as he pulled up an empty desk during lunchtime that day. "I'll be joining you for lunch again."

Yesterday's frankfurter octopus and heart-embossed rice caused the other students to gather around in anticipation of to-day's lunch.

"Ta-da!" Dai announced as he whipped out his lunch.

"Is that a ready-made meal, Mr. Watanabe?"

"Yup. Looks good, doesn't it?"

"Did you and Mrs. Watanabe have a fight or something?"

Imari, once again, jabbed Gaku in the head for his blunt question.

"Wow, Mr. Watanabe!" Takashi said with glee. "You've finally graduated from frankfurter octopuses. Way to go, man! I graduated from them after preschool, but…"

Imari pinched the top of Takashi's hand to punish him for making fun of Dai.

"Yow!"

In no time, Imari had Gaku and Takashi in a double-head-lock. Someone else then announced, "Ta-da!"

It was Lisa, pulling off the plastic wrapping from her own ready-made meal.

"You too, Lisa?"

"Yeah, well."

With no frankfurter octopi or hearts on rice to entice them, the other students gradually returned to their outlying desks as though nothing had happened at all.

Imari caught Lisa smiling to herself. "You're in a good mood. What's up?"

"Oh, nothing." But she couldn't stop smiling.

"Something's up with you and Mr. Watanabe. I just know it." Dai and Lisa glanced at each other—a brief, silent rapport.

"Oh, hey, Imari," Lisa said. "Remember that dress? Did you throw it away already?"

"Oh, that? Not yet."

"Okay. Is it okay with you if I have it? It'd be a waste for you to throw it away."

Imari looked suddenly serious. Her eyebrows furrowed—which always meant that Imari was deep in thought.

"Yeah… I guess it would be a waste. You can just take it home when you leave my place tonight."

"Cool! Thanks!" Lisa broke into a smile again. With her left hand, she felt around for her skirt pocket. Once she found it, she pulled out the piece of paper located inside and sneakingly glanced down to look at it.

Okay, so this black circle is me. And the space around it are the people that aren't me. That's why I'm able to be who I am. That's why I'm able to stand out. I'm going to make my dream come true, no matter what. I'm going to graduate from high school and go to an American college.

She returned the piece of paper to her pocket and reverently patted it. At last, she dug into the ready-made meal sitting in front of her. She smiled up at Dai. "Mmm. I love it!"

After the Prom

1

"What was she thinking, embarrassing Tomoro like that."

"Seriously. Like, how insensitive can Naomi be?"

"Not that you'd want to admit something like that."

"Yeah. I mean, dancing with the Benchwarmer?"

Every year on the last day of summer vacation, the third-year students of La Versa Academy held a formal dance. The students called the event "the Prom"—a nod to its American counterpart. La Versa was a preparatory school with a nearly 100% college admission rate. The Prom had been devised as a way of rewarding the students for their rigorous work in the spring prepping for their college entrance exams and, at the same time, encouraging them to work hard through the fall.

Today was the first day of Fall Term, and homeroom 3-2 was astir with the excitement of students who had come in later than usual—around 10AM—for a special homeroom hour. This was the first chance they had to discuss the previous night's events.

"Hiroko, your red dress last night was gorgeous! It was, like, straight out of Carmen."

"It's the most important event of high school, Shizu. You can't just waltz in wearing any old thing. But enough about my dress… what's going on with you and Fujiya? You guys looked like you were having a nice little time together."

"Shut up," Shizu jabbed back, blushing. "How about you and Yasuo? The way you were grinding against him was just... positively scandalous."

"Positively scandalous?" Hiroko burst into laughter. "You sound like my grandma!"

"Ew, yeah, you're right," Shizu replied, emitting a small insecure laugh. "I don't even know where that came from."

While all the girls were gathered in the right half of the classroom, the boys were gathered in the left—gossiping just the same.

"Yo, Fujiya, you were on fire, bro. The way you were all over Shizu? You're lucky none of the teachers called a foul on that."

"Yeah, okay, Yasuo. You even remember how many girls you danced with last night?"

"I don't know, man. Five?"

"For real? But you're trying to get with Hiroko, right? I saw you guys—her arms all wrapped around your back... her chest pressed up against you."

"Well, she better not be expecting anything," Yasuo smiled, leaning back in his chair. "There's four other girls on the menu, you know what I mean?"

The students were all lost in their own little worlds.

2

Naomi sat alone and prayed that this boring, claustrophobic time would come to an end immediately, and that no one would bother her about Prom. She couldn't wait for homeroom to be over, when she would be able to leave the classroom and be alone again. Then, like one long sigh of relief, she would be able to return to the quiet privacy of her home and continue studying for her entrance exams.

Naomi never stood out in any way and never felt particularly comfortable in groups. These traits had quickly earned her the nickname, "Miss Nobody."

Naomi could not understand how Prom was a school activity for which attendance was practically mandatory, and it annoyed her.

They should have Prom just for people who actually want to go, those who enjoy dancing and mingling. It's absurd that the school claims that Prom is part of a strategy to recharge our batteries so we can do better at our exams. I can't believe it's considered an actual school activity.

Ten minutes. That's as long as she had to wait. In ten minutes, homeroom would start and force everyone to shut up about their exploits.

Naomi turned her head to look at the clock at the back of the classroom and, as she did so, her eyes accidentally met with those of Hiroko and Shizu. Naomi snapped her look back to the front of the classroom—she knew what was coming. The two girls got up and sauntered to Naomi's desk, and leaned in, making a show of their interrogation.

"So, Naomi. What kind of dress were you wearing last night?" Hiroko asked.

"Forget the dress. Did you find anybody?" Shizu cut in.

"Find... find who?"

"You know. Someone to dance with. You did find someone, right?"

"That... that's not really something I'm..." Naomi was about to say that going to a dance in the summer of her last year of high school with hopes of finding a boyfriend was a frivolous indulgence, and the last thing in the world she cared about... but she stopped herself. After all, was it really so wrong to want to find a boyfriend?

Before Naomi knew it, other students were buzzing around her desk as well, dying to know who she ended up dancing with.

"Yeah, Naomi, who did you dance with? Come on, fess up already!"

"Is it going to be a steady thing?"

For the other students, there was nothing more intriguing than trying to figure out who Naomi's dance partner was. What kind of a guy would want to dance with Miss Nobody—a girl who grew her black hair straight without any attempt at style, and who wore the most hideous pair of glasses?

Naomi could only meekly protest. She knew that whoever

she mentioned would immediately become a target for ridicule.

"Come on, Naomi," Fujiya pressed. "What are you so embarrassed about?"

"Hold on, Fujiya," Yasuo cut in. "If one approach doesn't cut it, you've just gotta try something else." He laid a hand on Naomi's shoulder and announced to the classroom, "Hey guys! If any of you danced with the lovely Miss Naomi last night, please raise your hand!"

The classroom went silent, and a mild tension filled the room. The students looked to one another, eager, hoping someone would just raise their hand already and break the suspense. And then it happened.

There, shyly raising his right hand, was Tomoro.

3

Tomoro was on the La Versa baseball team—a team that maintained its dismal reputation as the weakest team in the region by losing in the first round of the summer high school baseball tournament.

He was sometimes called "Baldy" because of a small bald spot on his head that was unfortunately left exposed due to shaved heads being mandatory on the baseball team. He was never insulted by this because, well, he did in fact have a bald spot. He did, however, take offense to the nickname "Benchwarmer." This was because the previous year he actually had been a benchwarmer—

an *official* benchwarmer. He was the team sub who didn't get a chance to play in a single game. But he kept practicing—two or three times harder than the other players—and finally worked his way up into the starting lineup (though he was still at the bottom of the batting order).

La Versa was primarily a preparatory school, and most students couldn't have cared less about having a baseball team, much less a weak one. And yet, Tomoro had pushed himself, as though his life depended on it, until he earned his position in the lineup. After all this effort, it stung when students mocked him as a Benchwarmer.

Tomoro was determined to get rid of this nickname once and for all. And the best way to accomplish that, he thought, was to have his classmates—or even just one classmate—get to know who he really was.

Yasuo strode over to where Tomoro was sitting, leaned over and whispered, "Yo, Tomoro. How was Naomi?"

"Cut it out, man," Tomoro snapped. "What if Naomi hears? You've already done enough damage, blurting out that stupid question and forcing me to tell the whole world that I was her dance partner."

"Then what did you raise your hand for, dumb ass?"

"If I didn't, it would've looked like I was too embarrassed to admit I danced with Naomi."

"Hey, man, I feel you," Yasuo replied. "If I had to dance with

Miss Nobody, I'd want to hide my true feelings too."

"Why do you have to be so insensitive, Yasuo?" Tomoro's cheeks were turning red.

"What're you getting all worked up for? Yeah, she doesn't look like much, but she's got a pretty nice body. You know what? I bet you're remembering last night and getting all worked up in your pants, too."

"I said, cut it out!" Tomoro shouted. He jumped up and grabbed Yasuo by his shirt collar. With his weight training and baseball practice, Tomoro had a distinct advantage. But Yasuo was too hotheaded to back down.

The classroom erupted into chaos as several boys tried to pull Tomoro and Yasuo off of each other. Fujiya was about to enter the fray, but a girl named Ai stopped him. "Hey, Fujiya. I know this isn't the right time, but…" she said and proceeded to whisper something in his ear.

"Are you serious?"

"Yeah."

Fujiya turned back towards Tomoro and Yasuo, looking very puzzled. The other boys had successfully dragged the two apart, and the fight was drawing to an end. Ai, frowned, watching the debacle.

"What was she thinking? Embarrassing Tomoro like that."

"Seriously. Like, how much more insensitive can Naomi be?"

"Not that you'd want to admit something like that."

"Yeah. I mean, dancing with the Benchwarmer?"

Naomi didn't know if they were deliberately speaking loud enough for her to hear, but she couldn't stand it. She covered her ears and buried her face in her desk. She focused on the patterns in the wood grain an inch away from her eyes. Once she could hear the muffled sound of the classroom door sliding open, she looked up. The homeroom teacher had come in. The students scattered back to their own desks.

As soon as the noise died, homeroom began.

At last, Naomi was able to recede back into to her own little world.

4

Homeroom that day lasted two hours. The teacher gesticulated with urgency and spoke passionately in an effort to inspire the students. By the end of the class, his voice went hoarse. Watching their teacher worked up like this ignited something inside the students, and the room was soon thick with a mix of nervousness and excitement. Last night's Prom would be their last taste of fun for the rest of the year. From here on out, they would have to focus all their time on studying for their entrance exams.

When the teacher left the classroom, the students packed up to go home, possessing a renewed resolve to pass their exams. And still, the students, one by one, stopped what they were doing and waited—all staring at Tomoro. Determined not to let the attention affect him, Tomoro walked over to Naomi. Barely managing the words, he asked, "Naomi? If you're not, um, busy, do you want to, um, go out for lunch somewhere? It'll… it'll be on me."

Naomi blushed and kept her eyes on her desk, her lips pressed shut. Tomoro scratched his head. "Sorry, that was… a dumb question. I mean, who's got time to go out for lunch when we've got exams to study for, right?"

Tomoro, feeling clumsy, continued to backpedal. Then, without looking up, Naomi replied suddenly, "No, it's… it's okay. I'm not busy."

This triggered a deluge of snide commentary from the other students.

"Wow. As if there's not enough to study for already, they're going to go out on a date."

"Looks like last night's dance wasn't enough for them. They probably want to take it even further."

The tone of the students' teasing became increasingly caustic.

"If you think about it though, Miss Nobody and the Benchwarmer make a pretty perfect couple."

"Yeah. Like, thanks for volunteering yourselves up for each other."

Tomoro and Naomi rushed past the looks and commentary of the students and left the classroom.

They headed for the nearest restaurant, which was located in the upscale food emporium of a department store only a few minutes away from the school. The several hundred feet they walked felt like miles to Tomoro. Similarly, Naomi felt the minutes pass by like hours. All along the way, the only sound between them was the irregular scuffing of their shoes on the cement. It was only after they reached the restaurant and sat at a table that Tomoro finally allowed himself to relax.

"Sorry I picked out a restaurant in a food emporium. It's just that I've never taken a girl out for a meal." With the busy buzzing of shoppers outside the restaurant providing the only ambience, this was not the best place for a boy to make an impression on a girl.

"No, it's nice," Naomi murmured. She held up the menu up in front of her face—an attempt to avoid having to look at Tomoro. "And they've got all kinds of food on the menu." Tomoro took advantage of the time to look at Naomi, but he could only see her forehead and the top of her odd glasses. At last, he looked down at the menu sitting in front of him. A dreary looking waitress plopped a couple of glasses of water on their table and walked away.

"Have you decided?"

"Yeah," Naomi replied, the corners of her mouth curling upward—almost a smile. Tomoro called the waitress over and began ordering. "I'll have the spaghetti carbonara, beef curry, and the seafood gratin."

Naomi watched, eyebrows raised. The waitress mustered enough energy for disbelief.

"What about you, Naomi?"

"Oh. I'll have the carbonara."

"That's it?"

"Um, yeah."

The waitress shrugged to herself and then disappeared into the kitchen.

"Wow. You baseball guys really eat a lot!" Naomi exclaimed.

"That's all I'm good for. But from now on, you'll have to call me an ex-baseball guy. That summer tournament was our last chance at glory."

"Yeah. Too bad about that game."

"Well, thanks for at least caring."

His classmates never bothered to show up to his games; he assumed Naomi was just being polite.

"If the second batter had made his sacrifice bunt work in the seventh inning," Naomi continued, "when you had players on first and second with no outs, you would have definitely caught up and won that game. I mean, the score was only 6-5."

Something fluttered in Tomoro. Naomi's precise account of the game caught him by surprise. He had no idea anyone at La Versa Academy was that interested in the adventures of the school's baseball team.

"Um, did you come out to cheer for somebody?"

"N-no, I came to watch the whole team. No one in particular." Naomi had a hard time keeping still. She picked the menu up from the table without opening it and then just set it down again. The two remained silent until Naomi spoke, a sudden urgency in her voice.

"I'm really sorry, Tomoro."

"Sorry? For what?"

"For embarrassing you in front of everyone."

"Don't worry about it. Hiroko and Shizu were awful—interrogating you like cops or something. Anybody would clam up if they were questioned like that."

Naomi bowed her head. "I also wanted to thank you. For raising your hand when… you know."

"You don't need to thank me. But there is something I wanted to ask you… related to that."

"What's that?"

Tomoro took a sip of water. His throat was dry—clogged with nervousness. "Why didn't you go to Prom, Naomi?"

5

Fujiya and Ai walked home together. They lived in the same neighborhood.

"I feel bad about what I did to Naomi," Ai sighed.

"Why did you forget to pick her up?"

"I don't know. I guess I was distracted thinking about who I was going to dance with. I mean, I realized what I'd done on the way there, but I thought if I went back, I'd end up arriving late to Prom, and then I'd miss out on my chances to find a guy to dance with."

"I don't see why she couldn't just go to Prom on her own once you didn't show up. She's not a kid anymore."

Ai pulled out her cell phone. "On the night of the Prom, I accidentally left this at home. Then when I got back…"

"What happened?"

"I had over twenty missed calls from Naomi," Ai replied, her eyes welling up. "I mean she *really* wanted to go to Prom!"

"Well, yeah, I mean, it's the biggest night of high school. But, Ai, if she wanted to go so bad, she really should have made the effort to go, even if it meant going alone."

"But she can't do that. Naomi's not the kind of person who can just blend in with a bunch of people and act like she's having the time of her life. I mean, she'd been begging me for two weeks to go to Prom together."

"So I guess she even had a dress, huh."

"Yeah. She showed it to me the night before. A pink dress—actually a little closer to white—just really nice and simple. I thought it would look fantastic on her."

Fujiya attempted picturing Naomi in a pale pink dress, and immediately regretted it. He shivered—her dowdy straight, black hair and glasses kept ruining the picture.

"So she didn't make it to Prom. And on top of that, nobody

even realized she hadn't been there. I think that's what got her most."

"Everyone was bugging her about what she wore and who she danced with, and they didn't even notice she wasn't there to begin with." Ai stared down at the long list of missed calls. "Naomi really had a horrible day today."

"Man, I feel bad. I think I went a bit too far." Fujiya admitted.

Ai stopped in her tracks and spun around to look at him. "Wait a minute, there *was* somebody who noticed."

"Who?" And then, "Ohhh."

"Yeah. Tomoro. He knew she hadn't come to Prom, and that's why he raised his hand when Yasuo asked that question."

"That makes him a lot more considerate than me or Yasuo."

"Maybe it's not that he was being considerate. Maybe Tomoro was actually waiting for Naomi to show up!"

"No, come on! There's no way…" Fujiya trailed off, noticing Ai's serious expression.

"Even after realizing I'd forgotten to pick up Naomi, I just completely abandoned her. But if I'd done what I'd promised, she would have had a chance to dance with Tomoro. Oh, god, I'm such a horrible person!" Ai wiped at her tears with the back of her hand.

Pulling out a handkerchief, Fujiya attempted to alleviate Ai's guilt. "Damn. I didn't realize Tomoro had it in him. Not bad for a Benchwarmer, huh?"

"Don't call him that." Ai snapped. "He's been on the starting lineup all year. Naomi told me. He deserves a little more respect."

"Well, you shouldn't be so hard on yourself. You're a really thoughtful girl."

At last, Ai accepted his handkerchief and wiped at her tears. But then she shook her head, refuting Fujiya's assessment.

"Anyway…" Fujiya inched out on a limb. "Since Tomoro and Naomi must be having lunch somewhere around here, I was thinking you and I could go get some lunch, too. How about it, Ai? My treat."

Still wiping her tears and sniffling, Ai nodded.

6

"That sucks," Tomoro said. "I know how you feel, though. Believe me. I had to force myself to go there alone."

Even though Tomoro sympathized with Naomi, she didn't feel any better about what a coward she'd been. She rubbed her forehead. There was still so much she wanted to say.

"But I don't blame Ai at all."

At that moment, two waitresses arrived with the food. They hesitated at first, unsure of how all four plates would fit on the table, but after prolonged maneuvering, everything fit.

"All right! Let's eat, Naomi!"

Tomoro began to eat his food—though it was less eating and more stuffing his face. Naomi watched this uninhibited display of ravenousness in awe.

"I don't blame Ai at all," Naomi repeated, "because, I mean, nobody even realized that I wasn't there. How was I supposed to have fun at an event where nobody would notice me? I think if Ai had come to pick me up as we had planned, I would have had a terrible time. So, I mean, it's fine, I guess."

"A terrible time? Are you sure about that?" Tomoro had already moved on to his next dish—the beef curry.

"What do you mean?"

"I don't know, maybe there were some guys who were waiting for you to arrive so they could dance with you."

"No one was waiting for me to arrive," Naomi replied quickly with what, to her, was a simple fact.

"How can you say that when you didn't even go?"

"You know… what everyone calls me, right?" she asked. She moved to push her glasses up with a finger, but then stopped herself and grasped her fork instead. "They call me Miss Nobody. Why would anybody in their right mind want to dance with me?"

"Well, I happen to know a crazy guy who actually would."

"Really? Who?"

"Um, well, I can't tell you right now." Tomoro slid his empty plate away and started on his seafood gratin. He called to the waitress and asked for more water. Naomi sat there, confounded, still just gripping her fork. "And, besides, you know what they call *me*, right?" Tomoro asked.

Of course, Naomi knew. But she didn't want to say the name, so she took a bite of her food instead of answering.

"You've probably heard Baldy," he continued. "I don't really care about that one. I mean, I *do* have a bald spot. But you know what else they call me? The Benchwarmer."

"I know."

"But it's not true."

"I know. You play right field, and you're ninth in the batting order."

"That's right, you saw the game. So I guess that makes at least one person who knows the truth."

Just then, the waitress arrived at the table carrying a pitcher of water. As she noisily filled both of their glasses, Naomi murmured, "Is that such a bad thing? That I'm the only one who knows you're not a Benchwarmer?"

But Tomoro didn't hear. "Hey, sorry, what did you say?" he asked as the waitress walked away.

"Um, I was just… saying that… Ai knows the truth, too. She knows you're on the starting lineup." Naomi omitted the fact that Ai only knew because she had told her.

"Really? Ai knows?" At least two students knew the truth about Tomoro's place on the baseball team. He felt the deep anger that had been simmering inside ease and melt a little, and he began to feel a buoyancy… which made way for a bit of courage.

7

"Where are you thinking of applying, Naomi?"

"Me? Um, I don't know if I'd pass the entrance exam if I had to take it today, but…"

"But?"

"I'm thinking of applying to East Japan University."

Tomoro smiled. "Me too. I'm applying to EJU, too."

"Wow! What a neat coincidence!"

But Tomoro's smile quickly faded and he sighed. "Yeah, but I think I'd have a much harder time getting in than you. I mean, until just recently, it was all about baseball, baseball, baseball."

"I guess you would be at a disadvantage compared to people who aren't in any teams or clubs. So you haven't studied at all?"

"I mean, I *have* been studying. It's just that I've had so little time to do any studying, and after practice, I was just completely worn out. So my coach told me something."

"What?"

"Don't blame your life on the world you live in. He said life is about making an effort in the world you've been given. He told me that if baseball was getting in the way of school, I could quit anytime I wanted. But in all his years, he said, he's never seen anyone quit the team and do better at school as a result."

"'Life is about making an effort in the world you've been given?' He sounds like a really great coach!" Naomi surprised herself with the ferventness of her response.

"He is. If it weren't for my coach, there's no doubt I would have quit the team by now. And at one point, I was seriously considering it."

"When?"

"About a year ago, when my coach announced the starting lineup for this year. All the third years would be graduating, so the new lineup was made up of mostly second-year students. But I didn't make the cut."

Tomoro was one of only two second-year students who were kept on the bench. The other student was so crushed that he quit the team, leaving Tomoro as the only second-year student left on the bench—which was how he gained his nickname.

Summer vacation for most second-year students at La Versa was the time when they narrowed down their school preferences and began seriously studying for their entrance exams. And yet there Tomoro was, doing nothing more than warming the bench as he watched his teammates working hard on the field. This killed him—he couldn't focus on his studies *or* baseball.

One evening after practice, his coach called him into a class-room. "You getting anything out of this, Tomoro?" he asked. "Hanging around, doing nothing all day?"

Tomoro was silent, kicking at the floor.

"Because if you aren't, you can always quit."

That convinced Tomoro. He would quit. He looked up at his coach with dread and took a deep breath. Once he opened his mouth, it would seal it—he would be off the team.

But before he could speak, his coach went on. "You've come this far, Tomoro. You could give it another shot and earn a slot on the lineup for next year's summer tournament. Or, like I said, you can quit. But whether it's baseball or school, if you're going to do something, you've got to put your whole self into it."

Assuming it was his turn to talk, Tomoro opened his mouth, but, again, was stopped short.

"Think about this, Tomoro. Every day that you waste is a day that somebody who died yesterday wished he could have lived."

8

Tomoro paused, realizing how loud he'd been speaking.

Naomi just stared, listening attentively. The quiet Tomoro was so passionate when it came to his coach and baseball.

"He taught me so much." Tomoro concluded.

Even a great batter fails to get a hit seven times out of ten. But you don't see batters skipping their turn because they're afraid or embarrassed of failing to get to first base. That's because there's no such thing as failure in life. In fact, failure is about the only thing you can't achieve in life. Some people say they're unhappy with their lives. They're lying to themselves. What they're really trying to say is that they're unhappy about being so afraid of failure they won't even try. But they've got nothing to worry about, because the way life's been rigged, you just can't fail.

Naomi listened silently, engrossed—her eyes wide and gleaming. But Tomoro mistook her silence for boredom.

"Well, that got a little long-winded. Oh, you know what? If you've still got some time, do you mind going somewhere else with me? There's something I want to check out."

"Yeah, sure."

The two left the restaurant and rode the elevator to the fifth floor. The doors opened and Tomoro and Naomi stepped out onto the mall.

"Follow me," Tomoro said excitedly as he rushed towards their destination. Naomi hurried behind, eagerly anticipating what it was that had Tomoro so fired up.

When they arrived at the shop, Tomoro began looking around with the zeal of a little boy. Before long, Naomi found herself feeling a little disappointed. She couldn't figure out why he was interested in this silly shop. But then she considered her eraser collection and figured Tomoro would probably feel the same way if she were gleefully digging through bins of erasers. She supposed that different people found comfort in different things and, naturally, there would always be the inherent differences between boys and girls. And then she thought: If she ever started dating somebody, it would not be smart to go shopping together. But she cut this thought short. How idiotic for her to expect to end up with a boyfriend.

Naomi continued watching Tomoro. She wished he'd buy something already, or at least go somewhere else if there was nothing here he wanted. She didn't want to spend her time separate from Tomoro like this; she wanted to go somewhere and interact with him, talk with him. About his coach. About anything.

"Are you going to buy something?" she finally blurted out, a little curt.

"Oh, no, I just wanted to look around. I actually bought something here yesterday." Then he let out an awkward gasp. "What the hell?! He changed the price!"

"What do you mean?"

"These are now ten times more expensive than they were last time I came in!"

"Ten times?! How could that happen?"

"That's what I want to know."

What had only cost ¥300 the other day was now labeled with a price tag for ¥3,000.

9

It was only after talking to the shopkeeper that Tomoro and Naomi were able to understand what had happened. The five-legged stag beetles had actually cost ¥300 until a couple weeks ago, when a boy had come into the store. After asserting that the five-legged beetles were fine just the way they were, he had bought one, despite its missing leg.

The story of the boy with the prosthetic leg moved both of them.

"Well, I'm glad we came here," Tomoro said, as they began leaving the store, "if only just to check out that ¥3,000 stag beetle."

Naomi grabbed his arm. "Tomoro?"

"Yeah?"

"Um. I feel horrible asking you this after buying me lunch, but can I ask you for another favor?"

"Sure, what?"

But Naomi hesitated.

"Come on, Naomi. If there's anything I can do for you, I'd be glad to do it."

"No, don't worry. I'll… just buy it some other day."

"Buy what?"

As Naomi looked into Tomoro's inquiring eyes, she pointed back into the store—right at the remaining five-legged stag beetle.

"Is that what you want? Don't worry, I'll get it for you right now. Think of it as a present from me." Tomoro smiled a big smile and began to jog back inside.

"Really? Thanks, Tomoro! But I'll pay for the food and soil. Ooh, and a cage, too!"

Naomi was bubbly as a child as they walked home from the department store. Watching Naomi preciously cradling the caged beetle in her arms made Tomoro feel special. Here he was, strolling down the street next to Naomi, getting to spend this time with her. Wishing for anything more would just be greedy.

Ahead, he could see the intersection where they would part

and walk in separate directions. Tomoro wanted to stop. He didn't want to reach that intersection. But soon they were standing in that very place, his wish denied.

Wishing for anything more would just be greedy.

And yet, Tomoro couldn't help but wish for more. Something inside nagged him that once they said their goodbyes and went in their own directions, that their paths might never intersect again.

Is this really it? No, there's got to be something more.

"So, um, East Japan University…" Tomoro managed. Naomi turned expectantly toward him. "If we both make it in, I was thinking…"

"Of course I'll get in," Naomi replied confidently. "You just bought me a good luck charm." She lifted the cage with the stag beetle high into the air with an easy boldness that surprised Tomoro.

"Remember what your coach told you? 'Life is about making an effort in the world you've been given.' This little guy does just fine, even with his missing leg. And that boy with the prosthetic who bought the other beetle. I bet he's living a full life, even with that handicap. And if you think about it, if he had bought the other beetle too, I wouldn't be carrying him right now. So it *has* to be lucky. And if it's a lucky beetle, then of course I'm going to pass my entrance exams. But more than that, it's a lucky beetle bought by someone who works very hard everyday in the world he's been given."

Tomoro scratched his nose, feeling shy about why she wanted to buy the beetle so much.

"And I don't care if I'm Miss Nobody. I finally get it. What's important is living the way that's true to myself. I don't mind if I'm not the center of attention. All this time, I felt like such a loser for not standing out, but I don't care anymore if nobody notices me. I just want to be happy and optimistic in a way that's true to myself."

Naomi's passion ignited Tomoro as well, and he finally managed to respond. "You're right. I don't care if they think I'm a benchwarmer. As long as the people who know the difference don't call me that, it's good enough for me."

The two stood still for a while, just looking at each other and smiling.

"Anyway, what were you going to say? About if we both made it into East Japan University?"

"Well, um," Tomoro murmured. He remained hushed for a moment before decisively looking up at Naomi. "If we both get into EJU, I was thinking we could start going out."

Naomi gazed back at him, dumfounded.

"The Prom? I was there. Waiting for you all night."

10

Naomi did not reply. She began crying softly, and was unable to answer at all. Instead, she nodded once, and then one more time after a brief pause—as if one nod for each word in "Thank you." The relief Tomoro felt combined with the utter happiness and fervor brimming inside of him made him want to shout out loud. But he suppressed it and, instead, clenched both hands into fists in an expression of victory. He had long hoped to, one day, make this gesture at the end of a game. But his tournament dreams had ended without a single victory. *I bet this was God's way of telling me to save the gesture for the right moment.*

Naomi finally calmed down enough to talk again. "You know, I just noticed that you didn't get a good luck charm. I'm sorry I didn't notice till now."

"Don't worry about it. I've got plenty of stag beetles at home."

"No, it doesn't seem right. I want to give you a good luck charm, so could you just… close your eyes for a minute?"

"What for?"

"I don't want you to see me without my glasses."

Okay, some kind of girl thing I guess, Tomoro thought as he shut his eyes. He began to feel unnerved, standing in the darkness in the middle of the street with his eyes closed. "Okay, I'm starting to get freaked out. Is it okay if I open my eyes just a…"

Just at that moment, he was interrupted by Naomi's soft, cool lips pressing against his.

A few seconds later, Naomi's heels dropped back to the ground, her face bright red. "There. Now you'll make it into EJU."

She hadn't bothered to put her glasses back on, and Tomoro could see now that she had the most beautiful eyes—eyes as clear and brilliant as the sky that day. Naomi was hardly a Miss Nobody. She was shining brighter than the sun itself.

It was the first kiss for both of them, and the looks of the people passing by did not even come close to ruining the moment.

They did, however, feel a little embarrassed by the stag beetle, staring at them from its cage.

She's Always at Hearty

1

Dreams are colorless.

You might look at me funny for saying something like that. But the dreams I see every night have the monochromatic look of a sepia photograph.

"You must have really dull dreams," some people might say, dismissively.

If someone sees a rose in their dream, they're more likely than not to describe it as having been a "red rose." I'm sorry, but they're lying. Well, they're not *lying,* because they think what they're saying is true—they really believe the rose they saw was red.

It happens this easily. Even if a dream is in black and white, everyone has a perceptual bias that roses are red. So, when a person wakes up, their mind begins to color their dream without their being conscious of what they're doing. By the time they're telling their friends about their dream, the rose has become completely red.

It's because everyone is so oblivious to what they are doing that I have become so vehement about this—that dreams are colorless.

I'm a college senior trying to become a writer. I thought I'd use my three-month summer holiday to jumpstart my writing career. But it's been only two weeks and I already have writer's block. Eh, who am I kidding? Writer's block is what happens to talented writers who are having a hard time bringing the best out of their talents (that's what the owner of the bar where I work told me the other day), so I guess that just makes me untalented.

I've already set up the guy and girl who meet. That was the easy part. Also, if I do say so myself, I've done a fine job depicting the minutiae of a girl in love with a guy who won't reciprocate her feelings. But that's all I've been able to write so far. To get the story rolling, I know I need the girl to express her feelings to the guy. But I just can't seem to write that scene. I'm tempted to give up and switch it around—to just have the guy admit his feelings for her. But that would completely change the story.

Will I ever be able to finish this story?

Anyway, it's my last summer of college, and time is something I have in spades. So, during the day, I tap away at a keyboard, pretending to be a writer and, at night, I shake away at a shaker, pretending to be a bartender.

2

Reina worked at a bar called Hearty.

She had had been working at the bar for two years and, by

now, was well known and loved by the many regulars who visited. She was a skilled, attentive bartender—whether she was making a spot-on wine recommendation or a perfect martini.

And her reason for working here was pretty simple.

During the summer of her second year of college, she was looking for somewhere to drink with her boyfriend—something a bit classier than the usual pubs he took her to—when she caught sight of the sign: Bar Hearty. Neither of them had ever been into a cocktail bar before, but the sign and bar's exterior were inviting enough to coax the two of them inside.

Before they could even sit down, they were offered a pair of drinks by the bartender. "Sweet Lovers. The one with the slice of lemon is for the gentleman, and the one with the cherry is for the lady. The one with the cherry is also known as a Sweet Lady."

Reina took a sip. She tasted two layers—one of bright sweetness, the other of subtle tartness. They mingled and filled her mouth with a seductive flavor she found difficult to define. All at once, she really did feel like a sophisticated lady. She was twenty years old—surely old enough to start acting a bit more grown-up.

But as she turned her attention to the woman standing next to the bartender, she realized how much more she'd have to work to earn the distinction of being called a lady.

She appeared to be in her late twenties and was smiling warmly at Reina. She was clearly the owner of the bar. "The Sweet Lovers contain a substance that brings lovers together," she said, an inherent elegance to her voice.

Reina was impressed that a woman her age could be running a bar, and told her so. The woman broke into laughter.

"You're very kind, sweetheart, but I'm what some people describe as *shoro*—early old age. You'd think the dictionary publishers would have updated their definition of what constitutes 'early old age' by now, but no, *shoro*'s still defined as the age forty. What are they trying to do, pick a fight with me? Pick a fight with every woman in the world?"

She's the real deal, Reina thought. *A woman with class, looks, youthful verve, and wit. That's who men consider a real lady.*

Reina asked about the name of the bar.

"What does 'Hearty' mean?" replied the woman. "'Hearty' is the same as 'heartful.'"

"So, like, somewhere really warm and inviting?"

"Exactly, but you never hear anyone in America saying 'heartful'."

"But we use that word all the time. Heartful messages, heartful gifts."

"Just another case of bad English used in Japan—lord knows who started it. The correct word is actually 'heartfelt'—but I figured that might be difficult for Japanese to remember and, besides, 'Hearty' has a much better ring to it. Hearty can actually mean the same thing as 'heartfelt' in America, but, usually, if you hear it, it's being used to describe a bowl of soup, or a meal or something like that." She paused for emphasis. "All I'm trying to get at, sweetheart, is *why* do we keep using a bizarre word like 'heartful?' I mean, if somebody used the word 'crazeful,' what would you think?"

Reina blinked, not quite understanding, so the owner continued. "You wouldn't know what they're talking about, right? Well, of course you wouldn't, sweetheart—that word doesn't exist! It's 'crazy,' not 'crazeful.' We say 'crazy' just like in America, but when it comes to 'hearty', we appropriate bad English for some reason. Many of the customers who come in here don't even know what 'hearty' means, even if they do know a non-existent English word like 'heartful'."

Although Reina was embarrassed by her lack of English knowledge, the satisfaction she felt having learned this bit of trivia more than made up for it. She turned to look at her boyfriend, hoping to share in this satisfaction, but he seemed to be distracted by a woman sitting to his right.

"Now, if this were America," the owner continued, "I would have probably named the bar 'Hearty's', making it possessive, but I thought, why act like an American when you're not one? And besides, we live in Japan, thank you very much."

An American bar that was also thoroughly Japanese.

Reina found herself captivated by this woman. How great it would be to be like her, running a wonderful bar like Hearty, offering couples the chance to spend a romantic, elegant evening together with intriguing cocktails such as the Sweet Lovers.

I wish I could work here, she thought. She hesitated, but the impulse nagged—it felt right. So she asked.

"Of course, sweetheart," the owner replied. "In fact, you couldn't have picked a better time to ask." She put an arm around the bartender's shoulder. "He'll be going home soon to take over his father's business; finally realized that the dream he was pursuing was based on obsession, and not faith. Isn't that right?"

The bartender nodded shyly.

I don't get it, Reina thought. *What does she mean about obsession and faith?*

Before Reina could ask, the owner continued. "And besides, with a cutie like you behind the bar, I bet Hearty will see a boom in business. Nobody wants to talk to an over-the-hill lady and a scrubby young man."

"Scrubby? Aww." The bartender jokingly stuck out his lower lip.

Reina turned to her boyfriend to share her great news, but he seemed to have established an all too comfortable rapport with the previously unknown woman to his right. Reina watched as he ordered the bartender to get the woman a Sweet Lady.

That was her last night with her boyfriend, ruined by the Sweet Lovers. The owner may have been wrong about the cocktail's impact on her romantic relationship, but they did help usher

Reina into a new stage of her life.

3

Working at Hearty was the most fun Reina had ever had in her life. Every night was a whirlwind of fine wine, cocktails, and candid storytelling from the owner, whose name was Seiko. Still, Reina found nothing more interesting than the conversations she held with her customers. They each led such varied, interesting lives.

Some customers, shyly fidgeting with their drinks, would find themselves confiding in Reina—telling their stories of terrible things that had transpired in their lives. This made it tempting for Reina to tear up their tab and let them leave without paying a dime. Then there were the other types—the arrogant, contemptuous customers who never suffered a day in their lives and let Reina know it. These people were walking lessons, examples of what Reina did *not* want to turn into. Working at the bar allowed Reina to look in, to spy, to vicariously experience the lives of those who came in to Hearty. It was by far the best perk of this job.

Two years passed and Reina was now in her last year of college. She had completed her student teaching and, although it had been a trying experience, she was finally eligible for a teaching license. All that work she had put in to getting into the prestigious East Japan University would finally pay off. Knowing this day would come had been the only thing that kept her going.

It was Monday and Reina was working her usual shift. "Hi, Jun," she greeted the regular with her customary vibrancy. Jun raised one finger, then pointed at the bar. It was a signal to let her know that he would be sitting alone. He used this signal every time, even though there was never any distinction—he always came in alone.

"Sit wherever you want," Reina said, smiling. Jun sat down and relaxed back into his seat. Then he struck up a conversation the way he did every night. "So, how's Reina today?"

"Good as always. How about you?"

"I don't know. What does my face say?" he said as he patted his right cheek. Instead of looking at his face, Reina looked down at his clothes. He had the same dull blue tie he wore almost every day. Reina couldn't remember the last time she saw him wearing his red tie—the one that he wore when he was trying to get the attention of a woman.

4

Jun was a banker who started coming to Hearty regularly about a year ago. His first night, he had walked in due to a bet he had made with himself—a bet that had to do with his favorite movie, *Breakfast at Hearty's*. It had failed to make a splash when it came out—in fact, when Reina heard this, she assumed it was just a takeoff on *Breakfast at Tiffany's*.

He was betting (or hoping, rather) that someone resembling the movie's heroine, Sophie, would be working behind the bar. Of course, he lost the bet. And, that night, with a sheepish grin, he explained this thought process to Reina. Reina, put off by the story, looked at him with a touch of iciness. *What a dull, simple-minded guy*, she thought. The grin soon disappeared from Jun's face, however, replaced by a grave expression.

The change was not due to Reina's demeanor. Rather, it had resulted from a conversation taking place next to him. A woman was explaining to her date—candidly and without any hint of guilt—how, whenever she had a bad day, she took it out on her cat. In response, the man said, "You know, that's not a bad idea. I mean, people buy pets to make themselves feel better, right? Maybe I'll buy a puppy or something. Something cheap. I mean, I can't shout at my own boss, right?"

BAM! Jun brought his fists down hard on the bar. The couple, startled, turned to see Jun, whose fists were now aimed at them. The couple scurried up and ran out of the bar, their tails between their legs. Jun's eyes were brimming with tears. His fists were shaking with fury. Without thinking, Reina clasped his fists in her hands. She could feel his pulse, his strength coursing through his hands, and it caused her own heart to race.

5

Whenever Jun was drunk, he always said the same thing: "I wish I had a girl like Sophie."

But Jun's life was not a movie, and Sophie did not work at Hearty. Still, he kept returning on a regular basis, looking for the same thing. Reina could not decipher this mystery; it was like a fog that obstructed her view of Jun. It began to gnaw at her.

One day, after hearing Jun mope about this imaginary Sophie for the five-hundredth time, Reina decided to find the movie.

It was about a company executive, Paul, who went to a diner called Hearty's every single morning, promptly at 8:00 a.m. After eating breakfast, he would enjoy his morning coffee until leaving the diner at exactly 8:50 to head for his office. Sophie was a waitress working at the diner.

At first glance, it looked as if Paul spent his time reading the paper while drinking the coffee that Sophie served. But this was just a ruse. He would go through at least three or four cups of coffee every morning, each one carefully refilled by Sophie, and each time followed by a reverent "Thank you" from Paul. This simple, quiet interaction was his reason for coming into Hearty's.

Sophie, herself, had feelings for Paul, but she tried her hardest to dismiss them. It was silly to hold illusions of ever being in a relationship with a high-profile executive like Paul. So, she settled for the simple pleasure of his thank-yous and the smiles she gifted him in return.

A certain event, however, brings Paul and Sophie close, and at the end, Sophie nervously tells Paul how she feels.

It was just a very old-fashioned love story, with the look of an independent movie—perhaps that was why Reina had never heard of it.

Aside from her passionate speech at the end, Sophie was demure compared to American movie heroines Reina had seen in the same sort of movies. She had this impression of American women as being confident and independent. Now, after watching *Breakfast at Hearty's*, she began to wonder whether this kind of modesty was what men actually wanted in women, whether they were from Japan or America.

I actually liked that movie, she thought. *I could really relate to Sophie, and that Paul was kind of a dreamboat.*

But there was no one like Sophie working at Hearty. No bashful waifs serving drinks to customers. So what did Jun see in Hearty? Watching the movie had failed to resolve this question. Reina had often seen him chatting cheerfully with Seiko, so she deduced that Jun must be coming in for her. Case closed, she decided, and filed the mystery away in the back of her mind.

6

"I came today, because there was something important I needed to tell you."

There was a gravity in Jun's demeanor that Reina had never seen before. *Wow*, she thought. *He sure looks serious today. What could he mean by "something impor..." Oh my god. Is he going to...?*

The thought of this cinematic, dramatic twist caused the blood to rush to her cheeks. She felt her ears go hot.

"When I came the other day when you weren't working, Seiko told me that you decided to give up on being a teacher, and that you would continue working here after graduation."

Geez. That's what this is about?

"Yeah, so?" Reina replied bluntly as she served Jun a sidecar—his favorite cocktail.

"So… I thought it was your dream to become a teacher. It's your last summer of college; why give up now? After spending over three years at a school as top-notch as EJU?"

"Well, to be honest, I just realized that becoming a teacher wasn't my dream. Actually, I think I knew that for a very long time."

Although she was majoring in Education with a focus on Japanese Literature, she hadn't chosen her major specifically to become a teacher. It was too much to expect a 17-year-old girl who'd spent all three years of high school focusing on passing her entrance exams to simultaneously figure out what she wanted to do with her life after college. The typical high school student didn't even understand the difference between industry and occupation; how were they expected to imagine the work they saw themselves in? It didn't make any sense to force students to choose not only their school, but their major before getting into college.

This had been bothering Reina over the last few years. In high school, she attended La Versa Academy, an elite preparatory school where the focus had been entirely on achieving the test scores needed to get her into a prestigious college. There was no time or space to let her mind wander to the dreams she had for the future.

Even an independent-minded girl like Reina found it difficult to avoid the pressures of choosing a good university, and as she grudgingly toiled away at her exam preparations, she found her choices increasingly narrowing and, in the end, selected—or, rather, settled for—Education.

"So teaching isn't what you want to do. What about bartending?"

"No, I've got another dream. But I've also got to worry about things like food and paying rent."

"So you can't make a living out of your dream?"

"Not immediately. But that's all part of being a writer."

"A writer?! You want to become a writer?"

Jun's face underwent a schizophrenic series of expressions. At first he seemed surprised, then there was glimmer of disdain until he managed to force an expression of calm civility.

Reina expected this reaction. She knew what Jun was thinking—that she must have a screw loose, choosing an unstable career over the security that comes with being a teacher. She also knew why he was fighting so hard to not let his judgment show.

In the movie, Paul was not the kind of person who looked down on others because of their profession, and that was what helped him get closer to Sophie. It would be self-defeating for Jun (who hoped to find a woman like Sophie to fall in love with) to scoff at Reina's dream of becoming a writer.

Jun sipped his cocktail despondently, avoiding eye contact.

"Hey, mind if I have some wine, Jun?"

"On me, right?" he replied matter-of-fact, and smiled as if nothing had happened. He poured some rosé into a glass and toasted her with his own drink.

"I've always wanted to be a writer. I was the kind of girl who loved reading and would rather be lost in my own little world than play with other kids."

"But you were talking about becoming a teacher until recently. Something must have happened to make you change your mind." Jun would not let it go. Reina didn't know why. Maybe it was just curiosity. It didn't matter. Anybody who cared this much about her future deserved an honest explanation.

"My student teaching experience. Remember when I was gone for a few weeks?"

"Yeah. You were teaching at an elementary school, right? What happened there?"

"The president of the class I was teaching was this really popular boy—I mean, you'd have to be popular to be voted class president—and he taught me something I'd never thought about before."

"What. A kid?" Jun remarked, his eyes widening in disbelief. Reina took a sip of wine before continuing.

"This boy had a prosthetic leg. He was in an accident when he was in second grade, and he lost his right leg."

Jun listened quietly.

"What really got me was finding out that, until the accident, his dream was to become a soccer player. I didn't know how I should approach this boy, so I talked to my supervisor, and she told me…"

Before Reina had a chance to continue, Jun, who usually tended to be oddly wishy-washy with his advice, confidently said, "Just approach him like you'd approach any other kid. He's no different than anyone else."

Jun's answer was almost word for word what Reina's supervisor had told her.

Reina went on to excitedly explain how that class president had given up on his dream of becoming a soccer player and was now focusing on becoming a mathematician because he liked math. He wanted to, one day, win the Nobel Prize in Mathematics.

"Of course, I didn't tell him that there was no such thing as a Nobel Prize in Mathematics. That would have been cruel."

Jun smiled for a moment, then looked down at the bar, folding his arms. "What a strong kid," he sighed.

Reina allowed a moment of silence out of consideration before getting to the point of her story. "That made me start thinking about what I was doing. I mean, I had this dream about being a writer since I was a kid, and I just locked it away in the back of my mind. And what did I do instead? Get into college with no clue of what I wanted to do and announce to the world that I was going to become a teacher, even if I had no interest in it. But this boy, he had his dream robbed from him in an accident, and not only did it not bring him down, he even managed to find another dream to pursue. And here I was, my dream not robbed by fate or someone else—but by me. I was living a lie, and I couldn't forgive myself for that. That's why I decided to become a writer."

7

The next evening, Jun returned to Hearty. Even though he was a regular, it was unusual for him to come in two nights in a row right at the beginning of the week. And it was Tuesday— surely he knew it was Seiko's day off.

"You wouldn't believe how slow things are at the bank at the beginning of the month," he murmured as he loosened his blue tie. He wasn't speaking to anyone in particular, making the exclamation sound stilted. He wasn't under any obligation to explain his reasons for coming in, but his wishy-washiness certainly was in keeping with his character.

Reina imagined that Jun was one of those hard-working types who failed to make an impression at the office because he never bragged about his accomplishments. She assumed that was why she never saw any signs of a woman in his life, especially at the age of 27. Or perhaps that had more to do with the contrast between his rugged looks and his awkward personality. For Reina, it was this discrepancy that made Jun intriguing.

Jun had a special bottle marked with his name behind the counter, but when it came to cocktails, he always let Reina make whatever she wanted. Today, as she was considering her options, her eyes fell to his shirt. Reina knew what she was going to make.

"Here you go. Your tie gave me the hint I needed."

Jun squinted at the light blue concoction. "Hey! A Blue

Dream! You know, this was the cocktail you made for me on my first visit to Hearty. You probably don't remember, though."

Feeling a little embarrassed about stunting the conversation, he brought the drink up to his mouth and sipped. He closed his eyes, breathed in through his nose and let the minty flavor fill his mouth.

Speaking of dreams, Reina thought as she watched Jun enjoying her cocktail number 18, remembering her theory of colorless dreams.

"Did you know that dreams are colorless, Jun? I mean, the dreams you have while you're sleeping, not, you know, ambitions and goals."

"Really? Huh. I guess I've never noticed."

Reina explained how the world of dreams was monochromatic and why people insist that their dreams are in color. Jun listened and nodded attentively with his drink in his hand. He let her finish before he spoke.

"Have you ever heard the theory of invisible dreams?"

"Invisible? Not colorless?"

"No. Invisible."

The dreams one has at night may be colorless, but the dreams one has about the future can't be seen at all. Say someone has a dream that lies a mile away and they decide to walk towards that dream, even one foot per day. As long as they feel like they're get-

ting somewhere, they'll eventually succeed. As long as they put effort into traveling towards that dream, the dream will begin to loom larger over the horizon until, at last, they've finally reached it. But because these dreams can't be seen by the human eye, some people will give up along the way. You know how when a dream comes true, it seems to happen suddenly? That's because they're invisible.

"Wow! That's *really* interesting."

Then Jun smiled mischievously. "Just kidding. Reina, dreams are visible."

"What?"

"They're visible, and they've got color, as long as you have faith. If you can't see your dream, it just means you don't have faith in it. What *you* have is an obsession."

Wait a minute, Reina thought. *I've heard this conversation somewhere before.* It didn't take long for her to realize that it was the same thing that Seiko told the bartender two years ago, when Reina had first set foot in Hearty.

"What's the difference between the two?"

"Hmm... how can I put this? Okay... think of a monkey."

"A monkey?"

"Yeah. Now, picture this monkey with its hand stuck in a jar full of peanuts. The reason its hand is stuck is because it grabbed too many peanuts. It could free itself by just letting go of the peanuts. But because it has such difficulty letting go of the peanuts, it doesn't realize the simplest solution."

As he spoke, Jun clenched his hand into a fist to emphasize his point. Reina felt a powerful gallantry emanating from the fist, which felt as if it was being directed towards her. It was the same fist with which he had chased out the pet-abusing couple on his first visit to the bar. This fist, which had demonstrated to Reina the nobleness of men who possessed both kindness and courage, was now hovering in the air, just inches from her face.

"What that monkey is going through is *obsession*. The point where one becomes so impatient and fixed on something that they can't even see the dream anymore. And the dream does not *vanish*. It is the ability to see it that is lost. To me, people who say that dreams are invisible are basically admitting that their dreams are nothing but obsessions."

Reina listened, silent.

"Now, on the other hand, if you keep your dream in sight at all times and plan every move and give everything you have to achieving that dream—that's *faith*. People who don't have faith have no right to talk about dreams."

Jun emptied his glass before continuing. "Don't ever become that monkey, Reina. Obsession is for fools. If your dream of becoming a writer is something that has no shape or color to you, you should think twice about following that path."

Reina's mind raced. *A monkey clutching at peanuts,* she

thought. Reina was unsure whether it was the image itself or the urgency Jun brought to it, but the image burned in her mind.

"Well," Jun added as he smiled, revealing an endearing cluster of laugh lines. "At least that's what I like to think. I don't know if I'm the right guy to be giving people advice, though."

At that moment, a new voice rang through the bar, startling Reina.

8

"Hey, Reina? Can I leave for the day?" Standing next to an empty table was the new waitress—a girl with porcelain skin that contrasted with her dark, lustrous hair. Reina assumed that, since it was slow, she had been spending her time sitting and texting her friends.

I guess I can just deduct the rest of her hours from her pay, Reina thought. *No point in wasting money on someone who's not going to put in the work. Seiko will understand.*

"It shouldn't be a problem," she replied, formally. "Have a nice night."

Reina turned back to Jun. He was no longer facing forward but was staring back at the waitress. His mouth was agape—he was transfixed. Too stunned to think clearly, Reina's service instincts kicked in, and she found herself introducing the two.

"Jun, this is Emi. She'll be working here off and on over the summer. She's a junior at college, although we go to different schools."

Emi nodded her head briefly at Jun—not even low enough to be considered a polite greeting—but this did not deter him. He continued to stare into Emi's light-brown eyes. She looked dully back at him.

"And this is Jun. He's a regular here."

Jun bowed his head without saying a word, his expression frozen. The mood had suddenly become very awkward. Reina gave an exaggerated smile, hoping to cut through the tension.

"So, Jun? Do you want another drink? The same one, maybe?"

With an inaudible mumble, Jun nodded his head. But his eyes were fixed on Emi like iron filings on a magnet.

Just as Reina was about to interject, fed up with this nonsense, Jun managed to blurt out a few words.

"So, uh, your name is Emi."

"Yeah. Hi."

"Yeah, hey, uh, good evening."

What? Did he lose his speaking skills? Reina thought. *I've never heard a more bumbling introduction in my life.*

Reina could have said this aloud, and Jun wouldn't even have noticed. He turned his neck slightly and was able to take his eyes of Emi long enough to glance at the empty table to her right. "Are you always at the tables?"

"Yeah. I still don't know how to choose wines or make cocktails, and I'm not so great at one-on-one conversations. So, I serve groups that come in and sit at the tables."

"Right. Tables, huh." Jun was clearly wracking his brain for something else to talk about. Emi stood, digging through her purse, and didn't seem to notice.

"Yeah, so I'll be leaving now, Reina."

"Okay. Have a good night."

Once Emi left the bar, Reina mixed Jun another drink. As she set it in front of him, he pulled out his wallet.

"Wait, you're going home already?"

"Oh, um, yeah. I, um, must have been busy today, because, wow, I'm feeling beat after just one drink."

What happened to things being slow? Reina wondered, suppressing the temptation to blurt it out. "So, what do you want to do about this drink?"

"What? Oh, right, I'll pay for it, don't worry." He paid for the two drinks, added the service charge, then left the bar without touching the second drink at all.

"Really?! You wanted a second one! What was that about?" She was finally able to unleash her frustration in the empty bar. She picked up his drink, downed it in one gulp, and shut her eyes tightly. "Mmm. Just the right amount of mint, if I do say so myself."

You know, this was the cocktail you made for me on my first visit to Hearty. You probably don't remember, though.

"Of course I do, silly."

9

Jun came back the following day. What was even more surprising to Reina than his coming in three nights in a row, however, was that this time, he brought along a friend.

Jun looked at Reina, first raised two fingers (for two people), then pointed at the table with his thumb. Seeing this unfamiliar gesture was as unsettling to Reina as if a friend had suddenly started putting on airs right in the middle of a casual conversation. Reina's face clouded over.

"Hey, Reina," Jun said, "This is Osamu. We work together. Unlike me, he's not afraid of being aggressive, so he's on a pretty solid career path."

"Look who's talking," Osamu argued. "I'm not the guy who's got an MBA from America. The only reason the company's holding you back is because they know you're just biding your time until you've saved enough money to quit and start your own company."

What?! thought Reina. *An MBA from America? That means*

he must know English. He's probably fluent. You'd have to be to complete an MBA course in English. Now I get why he gets along so well with Seiko.

But why didn't he ever mention his MBA? In fact, he's never once mentioned anything he's accomplished. And why didn't he ever tell me that he's got his own dream? That must have been why he was so confident about dreams being visible—he's probably got the faith he needs to keep his dream right in his sights.

Osamu—the man on a solid career path—turned his gaze towards Reina and let it sit there. He wasn't gawking at her so much as assessing her like merchandise, appraising her. Reina, by now, had a developed a thick skin regarding lascivious customers and their stares but, now, she felt her skin crawl.

In an effort to avoid Osamu's gaze, Reina desperately searched for something to focus on. Jun's shirt caught her attention. He was wearing the red tie. This meant he was after somebody tonight.

Emi, up until that point, had been lounging at the end of the bar, languidly smoking and texting. When the two men sat down, she clicked her tongue and hoisted herself heavily out of her chair. "I'll be working the table, Reina," she said indifferently.

From the counter, Reina could only see Emi from the back. Worried about whether she was treating the two customers properly, Reina kept her eye on the table. She could see Jun grinning like a fool. *Well, at least she's doing the bare minimum*, she thought. In spite of (or maybe because of) that, Reina felt a ball of nervousness swelling in her stomach.

Seiko had told Reina that she hired Emi as a favor for one of her American friends, and that she would rather not have the girl working there. "Oh, well. I'm sure she'll quit in a few days, sweetheart," she had said. Reina had hoped Seiko's words would be prophetic. And yet, here they all were, two weeks later, and Emi was still an employee at Hearty.

Jun was chatting with Emi with a smile practically frozen in place. Reina couldn't understand what had got into him.

"Hey, Reina," Jun's crisp voice rang from the back of the bar. "We'll just need my bottle tonight, thanks."

Translation: I won't need your cocktails tonight, Reina thought.

As Reina looked for the bottle, she tried to understand this odd change in Jun. Just as she located the bottle, it occurred to her. "Sophie!" she gasped. She hadn't intended to say it out loud, but she did.

The resemblance was uncanny. Their facial features. Their tall, slender, model-like bodies. And, like the actress who portrayed Sophie, Emi was half-Asian and half-Caucasian. They could easily pass for twins.

I wish I had a girl like Sophie.

It all made sense now.

10

With a wingman at his side, Jun was much more at ease than he was when he met Emi the night before. Now, he was chatting away loosely, a completely different man. Reina wasn't trying to listen in on them—still, their conversation carried across the bar and into her ears, causing her pulse to quicken with every laugh that emanated from the table. Osamu was playing his part to the hilt, boosting Jun any chance he could. Reina guessed that, in return, Jun would be paying the bill.

Jun was doing his best to talk at the level of a girl who had no idea of the realities of holding down a job and believed that the world revolved around attractive college-age girls like herself. He brought up the routines of comedians who were popular with college students—god knows how he memorized so many in just one day—but nothing seemed to interest Emi. Her back remained rigid as a ruler, refusing to give into laughter even once.

In the movie, Sophie's demureness had been confused for frigidness by some characters. Emi, on the other hand, was simply frigid and only appeared demure to those who found her attractive. Reina imagined that, to Jun, Sophie and Emi not only looked the same, but had similar approaches in dealing with customers. In his mind, the two were surely becoming one and the same.

The situation was wearing on Reina. It was a drain on her energy that she didn't need right now. She cursed the whole farce and told herself to let it go and just not look at the table.

She cleared her throat and looked at her watch. She found herself nervously repeating this action in anticipation of the arrival of her own wingman. Finally, she arrived; Seiko's beautiful face looked even more striking than usual.

"Seiko! Do you mind sitting at the bar today? It's been really slow tonight. I'll even make you a drink!" Reina's voice rang out happily—she was like a puppy, ecstatic for the arrival of her master.

"Sure, sweetheart. Could you make me a cassis and oolong?" Seiko sat at the bar then turned around to survey the room. "Oh. How unusual. Jun's brought a friend."

"Yeah. He came in a little while ago with his colleague Osamu." Reina mixed two cassis-oolongs and handed one to Seiko.

"Thank you, sweetheart," Seiko said as she sipped her drink.

A lively conversation between Reina and Seiko followed. Reina listened attentively and found herself reacting loudly with surprise and laughter in admiration of Seiko with every story she told. Still, she would find her gaze drifting to the table—the center of the noxious fumes that still managed to make her wilt. Seiko pretended not to notice.

Suddenly, Reina caught Osamu, red-faced, grabbing Emi by the wrist and forcing a piece of paper into her hand.

What the hell?! Is that money? Is he trying to tip her? Where does he think he is, America?

Even from the back, Reina could tell that this was making Emi uncomfortable.

"Cut it out, Osamu," Jun protested, but Osamu just kept pushing Emi to grab whatever it was.

"Don't be a party-pooper, man," Osamu replied.

"That's okay, I'll take it," Emi finally said with a light bow. Osamu had apparently promoted himself from wingman to lead, and Jun now seemed to be playing a supporting role.

"Red as a lobster," Seiko said, stirring her drink, not bothering to look at the men. "That's what they'd call you in America if you got a bad sunburn, but I'd say we've got our own little lobster in here—and it's got nothing to do with the sun."

Lobster, huh, Reina thought as she looked at Osamu. *Perfect.*

Jun finally stood up, looking very disappointed. "Let's go, Osamu," he said, gravity in his voice. After paying for the both of them (as Reina had expected) Jun walked past the bar. The lobster, meanwhile, staggered this way and that with an idiotic smile on his face.

With things being slow, they'll probably be back again to-morrow, Reina predicted, her heart sinking at the thought.

11

As Reina feared, Jun and Osamu returned the next day.

While Jun was sheepish stepping into the bar, Osamu already had his game face on. The roles were reversed from the previous night, and Reina suspected that, this time, they would be sharing the bill.

But, almost immediately, both men were disappointed.

"What do you mean, Emi's not coming in tonight?!" demanded Osamu with such ferocity that Reina instinctively stepped back.

This was the fourth time Emi had failed to show up without calling in. Chances were that she wouldn't be coming in tonight at all... though she could be running late. Reina admitted as much to the two men.

"Dammit," Osamu spat out. "Guess I'll just have to wait till next month. Whatever. I've given her what I needed to—hopefully, something good will come out of that." Then he left the bar, leaving Jun alone with Reina.

They were silent. Jun didn't quite know what to do with himself.

"Hey, could you shake me up a cocktail?" asked Jun, not knowing what else to do or say. Just then, Reina's cell phone beeped—she had a text.

"You know... that could be from Emi." Reina looked at her

phone and, sure enough, it was Emi.

"Was it?" Jun eagerly asked.

"Yup."

"Is she taking the day off?"

"Yeah."

"Oh well. Let's drink anyway. I'll buy you a couple." Although they were not back to their usual ease, clinking their glasses got them partly there. The mood lightened a little.

"How's it going with your dream?" Jun asked between sips. "Have you been able to see it?"

Reina nodded confidently.

"Wow, that's great! That means you've got the faith to make your dream of becoming a writer come true. The way I see it, you're not really living unless you've got faith. I realize a lot of people these days seem to think of faith as this burden that they're better off without, and I'm sure those pessimists live a much easier life. I mean, since they've resigned themselves to a world where none of their dreams will come true, they'll never have to be disappointed. But I feel like that's a great slap in the face to those who come into this world with the desire to challenge themselves."

In her mind, Reina was nodding to everything Jun said.

"Now, I don't want you to get mad at me for asking the same question over and over again, but there's just one thing I still don't understand."

"What's that?"

"I think you've established that becoming a writer is your true calling, and working towards that goal makes you who you are. What I don't get is, why Hearty? Why not teach while working to become a writer?"

Reina had expected this question to come up, and she had already prepared an answer. "Well, by working at Hearty, I get to meet with all kinds of people. People who've led different lives and have different sets of values. I think that kind of experience can enrich my writing."

Her answer was only half of the truth. The other half was that there was someone at Hearty who made her want to stay. This truth, Reina told herself, she would keep locked inside her heart for the rest of her life.

"Yeah, that makes sense. But it can't be easy on you. Not everyone who comes in is going to be a peach. Like Osamu. God, that was a really bad idea, bringing him here."

Oh boy, Reina thought. *He's still not going after Emi, is he?*

"What did you think of him, Reina?"

"Osamu? Well, um, he was kind of... aggressive."

Jun ran over her attempt at politeness. "He's not aggressive, just *pushy*."

"Pushy?"

"Yeah, it comes from the English word 'push'. Basically, someone who really pushes hard to get his own way. I know in

Japan, we use the term 'aggressive' all the time, but it doesn't necessarily have a negative connotation in English. That's why I think 'pushy' works better in Osamu's case."

Then why did he introduce Osamu as aggressive? Reina wondered.

"Huh. 'Pushy.' Well, you're the guy with the MBA; I'm pretty sure there's a whole bunch of English words you know."

"Are you being sarcastic?"

She was. Reina furrowed her brow. She knew she wasn't being very nice.

"Actually, Reina... I was wondering if you wouldn't mind giving me Emi's email address."

12

"I'm going on summer vacation from tomorrow," he continued, "and I'll be going home to see my parents. Once I'm back, it's going to get really busy at the office, and I don't think I'll be able to come back to Hearty until next month."

"S-so? What does that have to do with Emi?"

"Well, you know, if I have her address, I can just email her if I can't see her here. I mean, you know how shy she is. She was too bashful to even give me her address last night."

Reina's heart beat faster. *He still hasn't noticed,* she thought. *Oh god, Jun, Emi's not the girl you think she is.*

Her hands shaking, Reina grabbed her cell phone and stared down at the screen. But she didn't say anything.

Growing impatient, Jun reached out for her cell phone. "Could I see that for a second?"

Reina pushed his hand away. "I can't just give you her address. What about her privacy?"

"Don't worry, I'll tell her that I got the address from you." Jun grinned, accentuating his trademark laugh lines. Reina continued to stare at Emi's e-mail, uncertain.

"No. I can't just give it to you. I'd feel bad for Emi."

"Come on, Reina, everyone gives their email addresses to everybody these days. You know, you're too serious, sometimes. You need to lighten up a bit."

Reina felt queasy, and she had trouble finding her voice.

"Oh, I get it," Jun said, and laughed lightheartedly. "You're trying to prevent me from contacting her, aren't you?"

"Yeah. That's right."

"What?"

"You've got me. I'm just a cold-hearted bitch. That's why I'm not going to give you her address. Do I look like the kind of girl who'd go out of her way to make someone happy?" Reina's eyes stung and ached from her effort to hold back tears.

"Wait, I never called you that."

The mood could not have turned sourer.

"Okay, look," Jun sighed as he pulled out a notepad and

scribbled something on it before tearing out the page. "Here's my address. Could you give it to Emi tomorrow? That shouldn't be a privacy issue, right?"

Jun put the note down on the counter, paid for the drinks, and stood up without once looking at Reina.

As soon as she heard the door close behind Jun, she slumped onto the floor and covered her cheeks with both hands. Tears began to stream from between her fingers.

Her quiet sobbing was the only sound in the still, empty bar.

13

It had not been a relaxing summer holiday for Jun, who now found himself completely inundated in work.

He never received an email from Emi. Considering the bad terms in which he had left the bar the night he handed Reina his address, he could only assume that Reina had never fulfilled his request. From time to time, he still wondered why Reina had been so reluctant to help him. But, by the end of the summer he had come to feel ridiculous over the whole thing—his imagining Emi as a character from a movie; the way in which he pushed Reina to pass his address on.

Emi and Sophie looked alike—it was true—but the more he thought about them, the more he realized that this was where their similarities ended. They were two distinct individuals with different personalities. Most obviously, though, Sophie was a woman who did not exist in real life. And yet, he had overlooked this fact and allowed himself to get carried away in a fantasy. He cursed himself for his foolishness.

What a shameless request he had made—and to Reina of all people. Although the last few days of his holiday had been blessed with beautiful, sunny weather, his heart was in a dark place.

Jun was working late into the night. When he looked around, he was surprised to see that he was the only person left in the office. He looked back at the computer screen to check the time. He would need to leave soon if he wanted to make the last train.

He shut down his computer and prepared to leave. As he heard the familiar hum of the computer switching off, Jun heard a different, unfamiliar sound: his phone's email ringtone. Jun rarely sent emails with his phone. Who could it be?

He casually picked up his phone, but the email he saw stopped him in his tracks.

Hey, it's Emi!

I got your address from Osamu. Remember? He wrote his address down and gave it to me the night you guys came. God, he just wouldn't let it go. If he wanted to score points with me, he could have just given me a tip, you know? Anyway, I wrote to him, and he finally replied, so here I am writing to you now.

To be honest, Reina tried to give me your address, like, maybe two nights after you guys came? I think it was a Friday. Anyway, I said no, but now I feel real bad about it cuz I could have written to you faster. Sorry!

But she was so serious about it and was all, "Oh, could you please write to Jun?" Like, whatever, just because you go to EJU, doesn't mean you can just order me around. And then she was giving all these weird requests, like, "Oh, could you change your email address before you write to him?" She's like one of those people who're so smart, they just don't make any sense, you know?

Anyway, I'm leaving Hearty and going to work at this hostess club. I mean, the pay is just sooo much better. Like, why am I wasting my time at Hearty? But this hostess club has this, like, really strict quota, so if you could come with Osamu and a few more friends, I'd really appreciate it. The address of the place is...

Jun snapped his phone shut. He was not shocked at the content, but was a little surprised at Emi's email address. It read "Emi", hyphen, a man's name, hyphen, "nlove". The moment he understood the meaning contained in the address, his stomach churned, and he felt a little dizzy.

Is that... Is that why Reina didn't want to tell me Emi's ad-

dress?

He could feel his heart beating fast—so rapid it felt like it might explode.

His phone emitted another email ringtone. Even though he was irritated at the thought of receiving another solicitation from Emi, he opened his phone and read the message.

Hi, Jun. It's Reina.

I'm sorry for writing out of the blue. I had your address from the last time you came (I know, it was for Emi, and I'm really sorry it's me writing to you instead).

How has work been? I hope you haven't been overworking yourself, and that you've been holding up all right in this heat. You were talking about how busy you'd be, and I just wanted to check in to see that you were doing okay.

There's something I need to apologize to you about. About that piece of paper you wrote your address on. The truth is, I never gave it to Emi. The more I thought about it, the more the idea of playing matchmaker made me feel uncomfortable. If it makes you feel any better, Emi kept asking me to give her your address.

I also want to apologize about not giving you Emi's address. I realize that I was being really petty, and I feel so angry at my-self. I know that you might not like me very much right now. In fact, I'm fully prepared to accept that you never want to see me again.

But I hope you won't stop coming to Hearty on my account. In fact, if you ever start feeling that way about Hearty, I'm willing to quit my job there. So please don't ever stop going to Hearty.

But if you can find it in your heart to forgive me...

Jun's emotions were brimming, and his thumb couldn't scroll fast enough. Finally, he reached the last line.

I'll always be at Hearty.

The very line that Sophie said to Paul when she finally expressed her feelings for him.

Jun forgot all about his last train and began frenetically typing a message. He was so jittery, he kept mistyping and considered calling instead, but he couldn't work up the courage.

Hi Reina, this is Jun.
Thanks.
Thank you for your sweet lies.
If you had told me Emi's address that night, I think I would have been depressed, and I guess that's why you played the bad guy. I also know that you tried to give my address to Emi, and

that she refused it.

You were looking out for me, but you were also trying to protect Emi. Realizing how selfless you had been the whole time has moved me to tell you exactly how I feel.

You told me once that you decided to become a writer, because you were tired of living a lie. I now know that for the past year, I had also been living a lie.

You've always been on my mind. But you were so popular with everyone at the bar that I told myself that I never had a chance. I fooled myself into believing a lie. As a result, I ended up losing myself in Emi, even if it was just a few days. But when I remembered how worried I'd been when I first learned you'd decided not to be a teacher, to the point where I couldn't even sleep at night, I realized what I had been feeling all along.

Three feet. That's all that separated us every night, but those three feet felt so far to me. Now I want to do everything I can to eliminate those three feet between us, to get you to the other side of the counter... to where I am.

Tomorrow, I'll be coming to Hearty with a gift. If you're willing to reciprocate the feelings of someone so awkward it took him a year to admit them—and in an email no less—I'd like you to have it.

14

The next day, Jun came to Hearty with a gift for me, as promised.

It was a bouquet of roses. Of course, I accepted it.

I was so moved by the roses, I clutched them against my chest, never wanting to let go. I wished that the roses would stay beautiful forever. But I knew that one day they would wilt, dry up, and rot away, as all things must. Then we would just have to grow a larger flower. A flower so big, it would dwarf even this bouquet of flowers that I could barely get my arms around.

Just then, Seiko called us from behind the bar.

"Reina, Jun. This is for you."

Sweet Lovers. One with a slice of lemon, the other with a cherry. Jun wondered why the two drinks contained different fruit.

Once I had finished my drink, I knew that the novel I had been having so much trouble with would finally be completed. My first novel would be a tale of love with a happy ending, just as I had hoped.

I was so happy that I was afraid this was all a dream. In case it *was* a dream, I prayed to God that I would never wake up.

But no, it couldn't be a dream. There was no doubt about it; this was the real world. All I needed to do was look at the roses nestled in my arms and the tie that Jun was wearing.

Both were a beautiful, vivid red.

And dreams are colorless.

The Business Card

1

As I arrived at the office after my meeting, I was greeted by the jaunty voice of my colleague, Michizuka. "Hey, Hoshino!" We called each other by our last names, which was customary in Japanese companies. "How did it go with Touchlink? Did you get to meet Mr. Nezu?"

I gave him the okay sign and then ran my fingers through my hair. I had cut it short in preparation for this day because it felt right—the nape of my neck felt nice and cool in the air-conditioned office. I had also purchased new high-heeled pumps. The crisp clack added an extra sense of conviction to my stride.

"Hey, way to go! So I'm assuming you got the…" Michizuka trailed off, also holding up an okay sign, his voice straining between expectation and nervousness. I set my briefcase on my desk then smiled his way and nodded.

"That's awesome! I knew you could do it!"

I suddenly became conscious of the other employees in the office and put my index finger to my lips. Michizuka, looking guilty, slunk over and whispered in my ear. "With Touchlink in the bag, they'll have to promote you to manager. You can count on it."

"You don't know that, Michizuka," I whispered back. "It's the guys at the top who decide." I didn't like talking about this in the open.

Still, I was sure that things would work out just as Michizuka had said. Touchlink had finally agreed to buy ad space in *Inspire*, the free newspaper published by our company of the same name. On top of that, it was a two-year agreement for three hundred pages worth of ads. This would deliver a massive boost to the company's profits. In fact, it was probably the biggest ad deal in Inspire's history. It was unthinkable that, after this, they would pass me over as manager.

As I thought about all of this, I felt as if my tailored suit—tightly fitting—was constraining my emotions.

"It's a done deal, Hoshino," Michizuka replied. "Remember what Shimada told you when she put you in charge of the deal half a year ago? 'If you manage to negotiate a deal, then I'll personally recommend your promotion to manager.'"

Of course I remembered. I hadn't forgotten—not even for a minute.

The entire thing had been my idea. I even created the presentation explaining how, if we managed to form a two-year ad deal with Touchlink, we could appropriate the profits to production and sales to increase our circulation by 150%. But when it came down to selecting who would negotiate the deal, I was put on the sidelines.

My boss, Shimada, volunteered to take charge of negotiations, and so I didn't stand a chance. I was 28, and had only been at the company for six years. If Shimada managed to close the deal, she was almost guaranteed to be promoted to director. In the meantime, I was ordered to assist her by creating the materials needed in the negotiations. So, in the end, despite having been the one to come up with the idea, I was relegated to working in the shadows.

However, two months into negotiations, Shimada began to lose faith in the project. That's when she decided to hand over negotiations to me, and she told me:

If you manage to make a deal, then I'll personally recommend your promotion to manager.

I knew what she was doing—she was taunting me to see if I could do any better than her with this project that had become a headache. But none of this mattered anymore, because I had risen to the challenge. And now, under these conditions, who was best suited to fill the recently vacated management post? There was no question—sales would happily welcome a new female manager for the first time in a long time.

"Where is Shimada, anyway?" I asked Michizuka as I sat down. "She's not at her desk. I want to give her the news as soon as I can."

"She just left to go to the smoking room. She should be back soon. But more importantly, let's talk about celebrating your promotion tonight. Just the two of us? I found this really great French place."

Here he was—at it again. Either Michizuka didn't know when to give up, or he possessed the ability to magically erase the memory of numerous rejections.

"I realize I'm telling you this for the *eighteenth* time, Michizuka, but I've already got a boyfriend. I'm sorry. And either way, my promotion still isn't set in stone."

"Don't be ridiculous. It's only the sixteenth time." As usual, he dodged my reproach with nimble footwork.

In reality, it was more like the seventh or eighth time.

"And be on the lookout for number seventeen because I'm going to ask you again as soon as you get your promotion."

This is how he always was. It was hard to tell if he was very persistent or just flippant. Truthfully, I did not mind, though. I thought it was one of his best qualities.

When I first started working at Inspire, I found myself on the receiving end of skeptical, competitive looks from many of my older female colleagues. They assumed I'd just been hired for my looks.

It was difficult for me to deal with—but I noticed that this malignancy dissipated as one after another of my female colleagues were taken out to dinner by Michizuka, who had joined the company at the same time. He may have been helping me out, or maybe he just enjoyed the company of older women. Whatever the reason, this transformation had allowed me to relax and concentrate on my work.

Besides, the ladies clearly enjoyed being asked out by Michizuka. He was tall, handsome, and a smooth talker. Who wouldn't feel good about being asked out by him?

"Well, I'll have to disappoint you again because my answer is always going to be 'no.'"

"I'm not going to take no for an answer forever, Hoshino. In fact, I've got a feeling that once you see how persistent I am, you'll be dying to ask me out yourself. Call it a hunch."

"Really? I have this feeling that your little hunch is going to be waaaaay off base."

We looked at each other for a moment and then broke into laughter.

"All right," Michizuka gave in, "I'll go back to my desk."

Once Michizuka left, I slid open my desk drawer, struggling to suppress my excitement. I pulled out my overstuffed business card book, hurriedly flipped through the pages to the T's, and carefully slid in Mr. Nezu's business card, which I had only just acquired at Touchlink.

I had worked and endured so much to obtain that card—an entire six months just to meet a senior manager. But I was confident that, once I established formal contact with someone at that level, the imposing walls around Touchlink would come crumbling down.

And today, that is exactly what happened.

I gave my back a deep stretch in my chair, imagining the lactic acid that had accumulated in my back—all the residue of half a year's toil—releasing and melting away. I was already beginning to feel whole again.

I gave myself one last pep talk: The management post was mine.

2

When I reported to Shimada about the Touchlink meeting, she reacted just how I expected—she was over the moon. And why wouldn't she be? As my boss, she'd be taking credit for this achievement. The first home run in the sales department in ages. I may have swung the bat, but it was Shimada who had ordered me to bat for her. The bosses at the top would never know the dubious reasoning behind her decision, and so the feat would still reflect well on her. I could already picture it—Shimada swaggering past the managers of the other departments.

But there was a twinge in her smile. This, I had expected as well. A wrinkle, a catch, keeping her from being truly overjoyed. Underneath, she was furious that a subordinate, someone less experienced than her, had succeeded in negotiating a deal that she, herself, had been unable to negotiate.

A look passed over her face at one point—a ghost of those looks I received when I first started working at Inspire. She suspected I used all the weapons that were available to a young woman like myself for this feat. She looked me up and down—and I imagined the ledger she was calculating in her mind and how it was adding up: a hundred pages of ad space for that petite face with big eyes and angular nose; a hundred more for those white breasts, pushed up tightly under the blouse; and another hundred for those shapely leg lines, ending in a pair of delicate, slender ankles.

It's not Hoshino's work that got her the deal, she seemed to be whispering inside.

Luckily, after six years, I had built up a thick skin toward this bitter appraisal.

Having been half-heartedly praised and simultaneously envied, I finally concluded my report. Shimada left her desk to tell the legal department to create the Touchlink contract. And just like that, my six-month-long project officially concluded.

Flooded with feelings of accomplishment and relief, I walked back toward my desk. On my way, I was stopped when someone reached out and tugged my arm. It was Michizuka.

"Hey, boss." He looked up from his chair and gave a charming wink. I was surprised to feel a peculiar urge to share the moment with him.

"Hey, you. Want to go to the break room? I'm still not letting you buy me dinner, but I'll be happy to accept a cup of coffee."

"Deal!" he said with a gleaming smile. "It'll be a coffee toast to the success of your project and to your promotion to manager." He began to get up, but I grasped both of his shoulders and pushed him back down.

"Not the management thing. Not yet."

He shrugged and scratched his cheek.

In the break room, we chatted for an entire half hour without me even realizing it. I decided it was time to go back to my desk, but Michizuka stopped me—he wanted to talk with me a little longer. I found myself agreeing—though I had to take a bath-room break.

After washing my hands, I wiped my hands off with a hand-kerchief and looked at myself in the mirror. I'd forgotten how it felt to smile so easily—so naturally. "Hey, boss," I called out to my reflection.

Once I managed to steady my heartbeat and relax my face so that I'd stop grinning like an idiot, I returned to the lounge. There, next to Michizuka was an unwelcome guest. Shimada was back from legal and was whispering secretively with Michizuka.

I paused and watched them from the doorway. I watched as Shimada stood up, pulled out a cigarette, and pointed toward the smoking room. It hit me just then that Michizuka was a smoker as well. I imagined that they were going to venture, together, into that dank, smoke-filled hellhole.

Yeesh, I thought. *Just thinking about breathing in all that nasty smoke makes me gag.*

I retreated back to my desk alone.

This incident would come to haunt me a week later.

3

I stood flummoxed in front of the company notice board. The words on the notice that had just been posted froze me in place, my hands clenching into fists. I was furious—panic-stricken. I couldn't believe it.

The notice announced that I had been passed over for the promotion.

I didn't understand—this wasn't supposed to happen. Who closed the deal with Touchlink, when even Shimada was stuck? And what about my track record? Over the last few years, I consistently ranked towards the top of my department. Sure, I had a rival who forced me to be competitive, but I was always either first or second. But none of that should have mattered. *I* made this unprecedented deal possible. That, on its own, should have ensured my top ranking. There shouldn't have been a sliver of a doubt that I was salesperson of the year.

But the name on the notice was not mine. It was the name of the only man who had ever ranked higher than me. He was the one being announced as the next manager.

My arms started to shake. My pulse quickened, and I felt like I couldn't breathe. The only things keeping me from driving my fist into the board and shredding that notice into pieces were the stares of everyone passing by. As I stood there motionless with doubting eyes, I could feel myself dissolving into an object of pity.

Out of the corner of my eye, I spotted a friend. It was Yamashita—the minutes taker for the boardroom. Noticing my confusion, he approached not with compassion, but with fury. The decision had enraged him more than it had me.

"Miss Hoshino," he fumed. "This decision. Are you going to just accept it?"

How could I possibly have accepted it? But I found myself unable to answer.

"And, of course, thanks to your accomplishment, everybody's talking about promoting Shimada to director. It's pretty much a done deal."

Of course it was. That was a given. I had known the minute she put me in charge of the Touchlink project that if I succeeded, she would be promoted to director. It was written on her smug, overly confident face. What I also expected was that, as the woman who made it happen, I was all but guaranteed a management post.

Yamashita then confided in me about how this breakdown of justice was allowed to occur, sharing the kind of details that only someone who had been at the meeting would know.

"There's one more thing you should know about," he said. "This might just be a rumor, and has nothing to do with what happened at the board meeting. A friend of mine told me that…" Choosing his words carefully, Yamashita conveyed this rumor, a scowl on his face.

My flesh broke out in goose bumps, as if a million caterpillars were crawling up my spine. I was disgusted.

As Yamashita concluded, my rationality—my pride, my will to maintain a sophisticated demeanor—all evaporated. I ripped down the notice and marched towards Shimada, the notice crumpled in my hand.

4

I didn't find Shimada in sales but, as usual, amid a cloud of smoke.

"Mrs. Shimada," I asked, "could I have a word with you? Preferably somewhere other than the smoking room?"

She glared at me distastefully, then put out her cigarette. She indicated that the conference room should be empty, and began walking down the hall. Michizuka was also in the smoking room—he flinched upon my arrival and not once did he look me in the eye.

When did the two become so close?

We entered the conference room and sat down at opposite sides of the table. Fighting the temptation to slam the notice on the table, I flattened it out and shoved it across to her.

"Mrs. Shimada, what is the meaning of this?"

"What do you mean, 'what is the meaning of this?'" she asked. She was chewing gum to replace the cigarette—apparently she needed to be constantly chomping on something.

"When I took over the Touchlink project, you promised that if I could negotiate a deal, you would make me manager."

Shimada gave me no real reaction but just stared, blank, playing with her gum. Her full, deep red lips produced a provocative smacking sound. Her face exuded a sort of glamour—meticulously made up to hide every wrinkle. I could see why some of the men at the company were enamored with this married woman. Although she had a daughter my own age, she owned a classic sensuality that a woman in her 20's could not pull off.

"Please answer me, Mrs. Shimada," I demanded, feeling my agitation swell. "Tell me how you can justify this decision." I could feel my eyes stinging red. Just as I clenched my right hand into a fist, maybe to bang into the table, Shimada replied.

"Ms. Hoshino. What were the exact words I said?"

"I remember what you told me, which is why I am bringing this up. If I managed to form a major contract with Touchlink, I was to be promoted to manager. That was the guarantee that you gave me, Mrs. Shimada."

"No, Ms. Hoshino. I guaranteed no such thing. What I said at the time was this: That if you managed to negotiate a deal with Touchlink, I would recommend you as manager."

"Then why didn't you?" I realized that my left hand had also clenched itself into a fist.

"Oh, but I did."

"What?"

"I told the board to promote you to manager."

I lost control, slamming my fists down on the tabletop. "Don't lie to me! I know that you didn't recommend me! I also know that when one of the directors who knew about my role in the negotiations brought me up as a candidate, you vehemently opposed the idea!"

"I see you've resorted to believing rumors now."

"It's not a rumor! I heard it from a colleague who was there!"

"Wait a minute!" Shimada cut in, clearly unnerved, lifting her hand up to me. She took in a deep breath and slowly lowered her hand to the table, shaking her head. I could only imagine she was buying time, attempting to think up an excuse.

"Why would I of all people try to prevent your promotion? Yes, one of the directors did bring up your name. And I honestly believed that was going to boost my chances of successfully promoting you to manager. But the other directors were against it."

She was lying. The other directors had been inclined to agree with the director who *did* recommend me until Shimada fiercely protested the idea. At least, that's what Yamashita had told me. Whereas Yamashita had no reason to lie to me, Shimada definitely did.

I was attempting to think of a retort, but my mind was so hot and swimming that I was blanking. Shimada continued. "I was really disheartened by this result, Ms. Hoshino. I really was. But when it comes to managers, the final decision is made by the directors. And this decision was made at the board meeting. If it makes you feel better to take your frustrations out on me, then do so. But the people who made this decision, for whatever reason, were the directors. Not me."

I hated to admit it, but she was right. Shimada might have done her best to block my promotion, but it was the directors that made that decision. And yet, this didn't change the fact that she lied about recommending me. I was not going to let myself be swayed or talked down—I was sure she had a reason to lie about her role, and I had this readied to use against her.

"You know, women always have it the worst. Do you want to know what I really think prevented you from getting the credit you deserved? The fact that you're a woman. Just a silly little girl getting in way over her head in a man's world. How can a woman possibly function as a manger? Most of those senile geriatrics on the board still have a Stone Age view of women."

This, again, was not entirely incorrect. The truth, however— the snag—was that these fossils had promoted Shimada to an executive post because she was able to take credit for a project she had left entirely up to her subordinate, whereas I was passed on. Two women, two completely different results.

My anger began to give way to exhaustion at Shimada's contradictory arguments and duplicity. I lost the will to hound her— it just seemed like the more I pushed, the more miserable I felt. I no longer wanted to lower myself to her level, so I decided I might learn the truth more easily talking directly to the man who did end up getting the promotion.

5

When I walked into the restaurant, he was sitting with his chin in his hands. He had a distant, disconcerted look in his eye—like he was trying to work something out.

I approached him. "Sorry to keep you waiting."

"No wait at all," he replied as he stood up to pull my chair out for me.

As I picked up the menu, I glanced over at him. He was studying the menu, his look somber. I quickly chose something near the top of the menu and pressed him to make a decision. Once we placed our order, we just looked at each other for a moment. Then, he spoke first.

"See? I told you my hunch was correct."

Did he think he could make this blow over by recycling this nonsense? I examined him—he certainly was lacking his usual breeziness.

"Hunch? What hunch?"

"You know. That you'd eventually ask me out yourself."

"This doesn't count. Besides, your other, more important prediction failed to materialize at all."

He looked down at the table.

"Your hunch proved wrong. I was not promoted to manager. So how do you feel about that, Michizuka?" And then, with a sneer: "Or should I say, *Boss*?"

Michizuka mumbled something inaudible, his head still lowered.

"What did you say?"

"I said I'm pissed off."

"Pissed off? About what? Things worked out exactly as you wanted them to, so why on earth would you be angry?"

"Wait a minute, what do you mean 'exactly as I wanted'?"

I sighed before continuing, "I know what you did, Michizuka... so you could be promoted to manager."

Michizuka looked up, absorbing the seriousness in my eyes. He turned his gaze away, out the window to the skyscrapers that dominated the area. His eyes blinked slowly, like the aircraft warning lights that flickered at the tops of the buildings, signaling their existence to planes that passed overhead.

For a moment, we sat in a thick, oppressive silence, until I couldn't take it anymore and cut back in. "You approached Shimada and asked her to recommend you as manager, didn't you? I've really lost a lot of respect for you, Michizuka."

Just then, our food arrived. A steak was placed in front of Michizuka. He immediately pushed it aside, its smell nauseating him. He set his hands flat down in the empty space in front of him and lowered his head. "I... am so sorry, Hoshino. Even if I had no idea that things would end up like this, it's completely my fault for being so stupid about what I did. I'm really, really sorry."

My foremost goal of the night had been to not lose my composure, which is why I specifically chose a restaurant at a luxury hotel to meet. I also wanted to maintain my image as a sophisticated woman—a promise I made to my late mother. However, faced with these lies, I could do neither. With the last sliver of my composure, I slid the plate of steak aside and pressed my hands onto the table in front of me. My nails began to dig into the table-top.

"You had no idea? Do you think I'm some kind of an idiot? I told you that I know everything! That the night before the board meeting, you met with Shimada!" My voice involuntarily became louder—and I could sense the sharp looks of the other restaurant patrons.

"I'll admit that much is true," Michizuka replied, halting me. My interrogation hadn't allowed him the luxury of worrying about what everyone in the room was thinking.

"I know someone who saw you and Shimada coming out of a hotel that night.

You made yourself into a prostitute to get ahead in the company—crossing that line knowing full well that it would block my own chances of promotion. And, on top of that, you slept with a *married woman*! And for what? Prestige? Fame? I think it's despicable, and I find you repulsive."

"Wait a minute," he cut me off. "What're you saying? How can you even believe that I would do such a thing, Hoshino?"

"After all this, you're still going to make excuses? You just admitted that it was your stupid actions that caused all of this."

"Shimada asked me out to dinner, and I accepted, which, yes, I think was a really stupid thing to do. And I know this doesn't excuse anything I did, but this was not the first time she asked me out. The first time she tried was the day you successfully formed a contract with Touchlink, when you left the break room to go to the bathroom. But she wouldn't let it go, and eventually I broke down and accepted." He took a long drink from the water glass sitting in front of him. "I'm guessing that, at this point, nothing I can say can make you feel better about any of this. Accepting her invitation on the night before the meeting really was a dumb idea."

"So you're telling me that it was Shimada who asked you out? That you didn't ask Shimada to recommend you as manager? That this is all her idea?"

"You still don't believe me, do you?" Michizuka was graver than I had ever seen him. I found it hard to believe that the regretful look on his face could be a charade. And the possibility that Michizuka could be telling me the truth began to gnaw at me.

I took a drink of water, slurping in a single ice cube. I let it sit in my mouth and told myself that by the time it melted I would get myself together. Then, I bit down, crushing it into a dozen pieces—anger and skepticism still holding tight to me. Michizuka noticed this and began speaking as calmly as possible

"Look, I'm not going to try to convince you anymore about who asked who out to dinner. If you don't believe me, that's fine. But I do want you to listen to the next two things I have to say. Please?"

"Two things?" I asked as I drank once again from my glass

of water. "Fine. I'll listen."

"Thank you. The first thing is that I am not having an affair with Shimada. All we did was have dinner at a hotel. In fact, just like we're doing right now. Just because someone sees us leaving a hotel, doesn't mean we're embroiled in a love affair, right?"

"Fine. What's the second thing?"

"During our meal, Shimada was insistent about recommending me as manager."

The obvious candidates are the two salespeople in my department who've consistently ranked first and second over the last few years: you, Michizuka, and Hoshino. But Hoshino's just a little girl. And so I thought, who's best suited for management? Who deserves to be promoted? And I came to an answer: you, Michizuka. Tomorrow, I fully intend to recommend you for promotion.

"That's when I realized how stupid I'd been—to go to dinner with her at such a crucial time. And so, I thought, I needed to talk her out of that decision. That became my duty—to do that."

"Talk her out? How?"

"I told her that nobody in the sales department deserved to be made manager more than you did. That she needed to recommend you for promotion, and that it was what she promised you when you took over the Touchlink project."

I bit down on another piece of ice. I looked into Michizuka's eyes and saw only earnestness.

I had absolutely no appetite, but I forced myself to stab a couple of green beans with my fork and shove them in my mouth, chewing on them as I chewed on the possibility that Michizuka was being honest. I turned the thought over and over in my head but my fury refused to let me go.

"You tried to talk her out of it and, yet, she ended up recommending you as manager instead. I'm sure she was looking for something in return."

Michizuka was about to cut into his steak, but he put his utensils down. "She wanted to sleep with me."

I nearly choked on my bite of green beans. Michizuka continued.

"You know when you charged into the smoking room today, looking like you were about kill to someone? She brought it up just before you came in."

I finally swallowed the green beans with difficulty. "So what're you going to do about it? Accept?"

Michizuka served me a stern look.

"Of course you will," I continued, cutting at him. "Nothing's free in this world, is it? She makes you manager, and it's now your turn to give something in return. Well, thank god for sexual equality. Now even guys can screw their way up the ladder."

I felt startled as my acerbic words hung in the air. When did I turn into this horrible person?

"That's low, Hoshino," Michizuka said, his eyes digging into me. "Even considering how you feel right now, that's low."

Michizuka was right. I needed to stop myself—it was unnecessary to continue persecuting him like this. I felt numb all over—I had turned into someone I couldn't recognize.

The conversation ended there.

I jabbed my knife into my cold steak. I had never eaten such bland food in my life.

Caffeine is supposed to energize the drinker, but I guess sometimes it has the reverse effect. As we sipped on our after-dinner coffees, we had managed to regain our customary calm.

"Do you believe me now, Hoshino?" Michizuka asked.

"To be honest, I'm just tired of the whole thing."

That was the truth. I couldn't detect any ill will in Michizuka's eyes or his demeanor, and I found that, by now, I had lost my interest in whether or not his claims were true. The central fact was that something happened when no one was looking. No matter how much I thought about it, or how it came to be, Michizuka was now manager, and I had lost this competition with him.

"I think I need some time to cool off."

"How? You're going to be working under me from now on. Do you really think you'll be able to accept that?"

A colleague who had once been such a good friend to me was now going to be my boss. I wasn't sure if I could ever be comfortable with such an arrangement.

"I… Honestly, I don't know."

"Then why don't you take some time off? Call it an early summer vacation."

This reminded me that I had been working nonstop since I first began at this company. I had only used a handful of my vacation days around New Years, but it had never occurred to me to take advantage of something like a summer holiday.

"Yeah. It's a little early, but sure, why not?"

"Go ahead. Take about a week off."

"All right. I'll use that week to clear my head and talk it out with my boyfriend. You know, he is so dependable, sometimes I forget he's four years younger than me."

The last fact just fell out of my mouth, but it seemed to lighten the mood. Michizuka smiled and relaxed into his chair. He reached for the cigarettes in his breast pocket. But, as he looked around and saw no one else smoking, his smile turned sour. "Man, it's like a guy can't smoke anywhere these days." Then, he shifted and looked me in the eyes. "Hey, Hoshino. I think I've got another hunch coming on."

"Again? Seriously, you need to give this up."

"Come on, hear me out. I know that right now, you don't entirely trust me. But I predict that, by the end of your summer holiday, you'll believe me entirely."

"Considering your sloppy record on predictions, I don't know. You were wrong about my promotion, and you were really confident about that."

But my sarcasm did not dampen his enthusiasm. "Don't worry," he murmured almost to himself. "This one *will* come true."

6

The next day, after lunch with my boyfriend, I went home and sat on the sofa hugging my knees, resting my chin on top of them. This was my favorite way to sit when I really wanted to think something out.

I spent the entire meal throwing an erratic series of emotions at my boyfriend. He absorbed them with admiration, praise, and sadness—in just that order. First, there was admiration for my initiative and mental strength, riding into Touchlink all on my own. He congratulated me in a very gentle, nurturing manner. Then he expressed anger at the obvious injustice of my being passed over in spite of being the one who secured the Touchlink deal.

But the next wounding thing he said caught me by surprise.

He said that, while he knew I had spent six years working in the free newspaper industry, he had a lot of doubt about my future in it. This was something he'd been thinking for a long time, but he did not want to trespass or tell me how to run my life. He wanted to respect the choices I had made... which was why he had kept silent all this time.

Graduating from an American college meant that, when I came back to Japan, I was immediately confronted with a tough job market. Big companies still recruited most of their employees from major Japanese universities, so I didn't have the luxury of being choosy. I had no prior experience in the free newspaper industry, but my time in America helped me develop my debating skills and, by extension, my negotiating skills. And, surely, I could use those skills in sales. I figured, as long as I was in sales, it didn't matter to me what industry I worked in.

As luck would have it, my four years in America did prove valuable here, and it wasn't long before I landed my "dream job" working in sales at Inspire—the largest free newspaper company in Japan.

I met my boyfriend two years later. He was laying flowers at the sight of the bus accident that had killed my mother. For the first time in my life, I experienced déjà vu. I had this inkling, this feeling that I had met him somewhere before—though I was sure this was the first time I had ever met him. We started dating soon after that chance encounter. He was still in university at the time.

And now, an entire four years later, he had been forthright with me, speaking from his heart, pleading for me to think about whether my job, the people I associated with, and the life I was leading were really making me a complete, happy person.

I rolled my chin from side to side, thinking about the dream I once had, as far back as when I was a third-year student in high school, exhilarated by the idea of traveling to America. It wasn't a dream of working in sales at a free newspaper company—that was for certain. But as the work piled up, the demon in me that hated to lose began to take over. Under the control of my ego, the dream I once had began to blur, and fade a little bit each day. And in the end, everything was eclipsed by my desire to climb the ladder at Inspire.

Initially, I wanted to become an interpreter, which was why I chose an American college in the first place. But after spending time in America, my dreams began to transform. I discovered the joys of being able to speak English and the wonders of living as a global citizen. I learned of new and different values and viewpoints by being able to communicate with people from different countries. A desire grew inside of me to share these discoveries with others as well. That's when I began to seriously consider starting an English school when I returned to Japan.

But there was another part of me that had put a stop to that dream. *How are you going to beat the competition*, this other part asked. *Where are you going to get the money from?*

These were not trivial questions. But didn't such competition indicate how much demand there was for this service? Still, if I wanted to rent a large office, recruit hundreds of students, and hire dozens of teachers, I would need a huge amount of money. But where was the need for that? If I wanted to, I could simply start up the business in a simple studio flat, with myself as the only teacher. If the students liked my classes, word of mouth would bring me more students. And if I started to become overwhelmed with applicants, then I would start hiring teachers so I could focus on the business side of things.

I had even calculated how much I could earn by teaching English on my own. But no matter how I construed the figures to reflect best-case scenarios, it was always far less than what the established English school chains were making. Once I factored in the amount of administrative work I would need to do, I realized I might not even break even. This was the one thing I desperately wanted to avoid—I was so afraid of being poor. Even the remote possibility terrified me.

At that moment, a picture materialized in my mind. I saw a cramped, dank flat where a single teacher was struggling to teach English to only a handful of students who were having difficulty grasping the language. Then I saw my face on this teacher—I looked so worn out and dowdy. This is not what I had gone to America for, I told myself. Then I envisioned a woman, slick and confident in a sharp suit, charging down the corporate path. This was the image I should be pursuing.

This was the very image that my boyfriend had just argued I had been all wrong about. He didn't have anything against working for a major corporation, but he was adamant that I was not the type of woman who could live her life clinging onto a single company.

It was what he had said next that really stuck with me.

7

I don't want to sound full of myself, but I'm a pretty gifted salesperson. My record speaks for itself.

But when my boyfriend asked whether that was a true reflection of my own efforts, it made me stop short.

And it got me thinking: Why was I so determined to meet with Mr. Nezu? It was not because I had seen something in him that was compelling. It was simply because he was the boss. He was a boss at Touchlink, and that's why I wanted to earn his business card.

The proof is contained in the very arrangement of my business card book. I didn't put Nezu's card under "N"; I put it under "T" for Touchlink.

I'm sure that those at Touchlink who received my card did the exact same thing. Of course, they would not have placed it under "H" for Hoshino. They almost certainly placed it under "I" for Inspire. They didn't agree to negotiate a contract with me, Hoshino. They wanted to broker a contract with Hoshino from Inspire. It was such an obvious point, and yet I had never taken a moment to examine the idea.

Every businessperson in Japan worth their salt carries around business cards. When it comes to sales, in particular, nothing can even happen without first offering your business card. Although ostensibly a tool for identifying yourself to clients and giving them a direct line to your company, what's the most important information written on it? Isn't it the company name? My name, printed right there in the middle of the card, is actually little more than a footnote.

As I mulled over the true nature of a business card, my brain began to feel fried. So, I walked over to pour myself some coffee—iced coffee, perfect for the sweltering day.

First, I added a bit of simple syrup. Then I poured in some milk, creating a white whirlpool in the middle of the glass. As I gazed into the center of that vortex, I lamented my inability to take my coffee black, even at this age.

Suddenly, I thought I saw a smiling face floating in the swirling amber liquid. Was it a trick of the eye? No, I'm positive. It was a face I knew very well.

I rushed back to my room to open my desk drawer. I stuck my hand deep into the drawer and fished around until I found what I was looking for. Barely grasping it between two fingers, I pulled it out.

It had been years since I had last looked at it, and I had almost forgotten it existed. But there it was, right where I had left it.

The card was like any other business card, featuring a name and work address on the front. I flipped it over to the other side, which was blank except for a black circle drawn in the center.

If the surrounding area were black, this black circle would cease to exist. In other words, the absolute condition for a black circle to exist is for it to be in contact with something that isn't black.

The conversation from thirteen years ago began to replay in my mind as if it had only happened yesterday.

Okay, so this black circle is me. And the space around it are the people that aren't me. That's why I'm able to be who I am. That's why I'm able to stand out.

Just an ordinary black circle, drawn with a pen. But to me, it was far more significant.

I remembered Mr. Watanabe's embarrassed look when he was explaining the black circle to me, but I had understood what he was trying to convey. That's why I had hung onto the business card for all this time.

When had I become so reliant on business cards, excruciatingly conscious of my company name and breaking my back to hold a more prominent title?

Without realizing it, I had begun blending in with the area around that black circle. And now I knew I had to find my way back to maintaining my identity—like this black circle. To be who I am. To be Lisa Hoshino.

As I stared at the circle, it seemed to rise up like it was embossed, demanding my attention.

For the last six years, I had lived by the front of my business card. From now on, I would have to live by the back of it. Running the tip of my finger over the black circle, I knew what I needed to do.

8

"Did you hear? Hoshino's quitting!"

"I know! I guess she must have been really upset about being passed over for promotion."

"Well, obviously. It's going to be a lot harder now for her to act like she's above everyone else."

"That still doesn't explain her outfit today. I thought she was going to change once she got here, but I guess not. What happened to those suits she's always showing off?"

My colleagues were gossiping about me in hushed tones, but I could hear them perfectly. It was like they wanted me to hear. One person's misfortune is another person's honey.

Still, I was surprised at how fast the news spread. It would make perfect sense that Shimada leaked the information as soon as I turned in my resignation. The only information I included on the paper were two short sentences explaining my reasoning, the date, and my name.

Apparently, that was more than enough to incite Shimada to advertise the news to anyone who would listen.

I decided to quit as soon as my early summer vacation ended. There would be a lot of work in the coming days to get my replacement up to speed, so I was glad everything related to Touch-link was already done. I would not be leaving behind any projects with loose ends. Once the handover was complete, I would be able to vanish from this office as though I had never even existed.

The first thing I decided to do was organize my things. My desk and cabinet were packed with materials and resources that were once priceless to me and were now, quite literally, garbage. There was an instinctive moment where I had the impulse to take these papers home for safekeeping. I laughed this off and fed them to the shredder. With every grinding whir, I felt increasing lightness.

By evening, I had cleaned up most of my things. It had taken me six years to amass all of it, and yet it only took a few hours to destroy everything. Only the hefty business card book stood out from everything else, obvious, sitting atop my desk for all to see. The value it once held for me had also ceased to exist. Tomorrow, I would hand it over to the others in my department without a trace of regret.

There was only one perplexing thing. Michizuka, who usually poked his nose into my affairs, was strangely silent about my leaving. He wasn't ignoring me; we bantered about the usual nonsense he brought up. But he never brought up my resignation. It didn't seem like he was avoiding the subject—only like he was, plainly, not interested.

Perhaps, with me out of the rat race, my future was no longer a concern of his. And that was fine. I no longer felt bitter or despondent; I genuinely wished him the best.

Good luck, boss.

Finally, my last day at the company arrived. I was exhausted from the farewell party my colleagues held for me the previous night, but with my handover duties complete, I was now only an hour away from being a free woman. With nothing else on my plate, I lazily stared up at the clock, waiting for the little hand to reach five. At 5:00 p.m., one challenge would end, and another would begin.

Suddenly, one of my female colleagues darted into the office, her face pale in disbelief, and began hysterically babbling to one of her friends.

"Mr. Michizuka just handed in his resignation!"

"What?!" replied her friend. "Tell me you're joking!"

The room was suddenly clamorous with anxiety.

"Are you kidding me?!" one asked.

"I'm serious!" the first one replied. "I was just walking past the conference room and overheard Mr. Michizuka talking to Mrs. Shimada!"

Of course, there was no one in the room more surprised than me. Why would he pull something like that? Michizuka was good at his job and would have made a fantastic manager.

"She won't accept it," one of the women insisted. "There is no way that Mrs. Shimada would accept his resignation!"

"No, you're right," a male colleague replied. Soon, all the men and women in the room—my colleagues for just one more hour—agreed about this notion. I agreed as well. There was no chance that Shimada would allow Michizuka to quit, not after he had been made manager. His resignation would have far greater consequences than mine, especially considering the shady circumstances under which he unwittingly won Shimada's favor.

The frantic speculations, however, were soon put to rest with the arrival of Michizuka and Shimada themselves—and the looks on their faces. It was evident how the meeting had ended.

"Is it true that you're quitting, Mr. Michizuka?"

"Please reconsider, Mr. Michizuka! It's not too late!"

Confusion quickly circulated through the department—everyone on the verge of panic. And, as if to answer, Michizuka sprang forth from where he was standing—kicking his foot back as if throwing sand up into Shimada's face—and strode past the befuddled stares towards me.

"So, Hoshino. Do you believe me now?"

"B-believe what?" I couldn't speak properly—it was as if someone had a hold of my jugular.

"I told you that I wasn't the kind of guy who'd do anything to become manager. That you deserved the promotion more than I did."

"But... but why does that mean you have to quit?"

"I don't know. Pride, maybe? I mean, being handed a management position based on something I didn't do? How am I supposed to work here knowing I'm wearing a crown I don't deserve? My pride won't allow it." I continued to listen in awe. "Besides, I could give a damn about a company that treats its employees so poorly."

"But you're good at your job, Michizuka. Every month, it was always you and me at the top."

"And sometimes I came in first. But Touchlink? That was in a whole other league, Hoshino. I can't claim to be first anymore. Even if I stayed, I'd know that I would always be second. That I could never beat you at this game." He paused for effect before continuing. "So how 'bout it, Hoshino? Do you believe me now?"

I nodded without saying a word. I felt something warm in the corners of my eyes and realized I was crying. The tears had started coming and there was nothing I could do about it.

"See? I told you I had a hunch."

"Hunch? What Hunch?"

"You know, at the restaurant. That after your summer vacation, you'd start believing in me."

This time, his prediction had indeed come true.

9

That night, I had dinner with Michizuka at the same restaurant we had previously met.

"Weren't you surprised when I quit?" I asked.

"Not really," Michizuka replied with a warm smile. "I figured that would be your decision after thinking it over during your vacation. I could just tell."

"How?"

"Remember at that company reception for new employees when you told me that you eventually wanted to go independent?" He paused, searching my face. "Wait, don't tell me you'd forgotten about that?"

I had forgotten.

"You know, when you were talking about how the size of a company and having a fancy title didn't mean all that much to you? Don't you remember?"

I didn't remember.

"Anyway, I remembered that, and I thought, 'hey, maybe this nasty turn of events will help her return to the mindset she used to have.'"

I hated to admit it, but there were times when Michizuka was impressively insightful.

The steak that had been so flavorless last time was delicious tonight. With our appetites satiated, we enjoyed our post-meal coffees—Michizuka once again looking like he couldn't function without a cigarette in his mouth.

I decided to help him out by bringing up a topic he'd be interested in, and immediately I thought of the black circle. He listened attentively and, halfway through, asked to see the card.

I pulled it out of my purse—its new home after having been tucked away like a good luck charm for years—and handed it to

Michizuka, who grabbed it giddily. Watching him study it with such reverence made something soften inside me, and I began to speak, letting something slip that I had been holding back.

"Wow," he replied. "An English school." He paused, on the edge of saying something, then didn't, avoiding and talking all around it. "I knew you'd go independent sooner or later."

What did he want to say so badly? I'd never seen such circumvention from him before. Just as I was beginning to regret my haste in blabbing about my future plans on my last day on the job, Michizuka halted, leaned forward and said, "Hoshino. Let me work at your school." He bowed his head until it was touching the table. "Please. Let me do this for you."

This definitely threw a twist into my plans. I intended to start alone and slowly build up my business. I had not even started recruiting students yet—there would be no money coming with which I would be able to pay him.

"You can pay me whenever you can. It's not a big deal since I've saved up quite a bit. And besides, I've got all the time in the world right now, seeing as I'm unemployed."

"Yeah, but... do you even know how to teach English? I mean, I know you lived abroad for a while, but..."

"Again, my offer is sincere. Please, Hoshino." This wasn't the usual playful Michizuka. His eyes were serious.

"Are you sure you want to work for me? It's not too late to go back to Inspire, you know? If worse comes to worst, you'll be looking at a salary that's five or six times less than what you would make there."

"Sure, but that's only for now, right? You don't know what's going to happen in the future. Besides, you've given me an idea of the kind of guy I want to be."

"What do you mean?"

"That black circle. That's who I want to be."

Before I had recruited a single student, I already had my first employee.

10

"Listen. I've got this great idea for a company name," Michizuka said, giddy. "Well, school name."

"Really? Tell me."

"Okay. So 'Hoshi' is 'star' in English, and 'Michi' is 'road' in English, right? So I was thinking, what about Roadstar?"

"Wait, how does your name become part of the equation?"

"Think about it. It'll be like Hewlett-Packard. And that can't be a bad thing, right?"

"Yeah, but it sounds like a car name, and… Wait a minute, why does your name come before mine?!"

"Whoops! Sorry about that, boss."

We doubled over, laughing. The other customers began to stare as though we were from another planet—but we kept laughing, oblivious. Our laughter consumed us so much that we were out of breath, and, finally, we calmed down.

"I thought I was going to dislocate my jaw, I was laughing so hard." I said, catching my breath.

"My bad," Michizuka said. "Oh, before I forget, there's something that I'm worried about."

"What? I haven't even discussed my strategy yet."

"It's not that. It's about your boyfriend. The guy you've brought up seven times—no wait, the other day makes it eight times."

I found it interesting that he could recall the exact number.

"Is he going to be all right with us spending so much time together at the school? I mean, he's still in grad school, right?"

"He'll be fine. He'll be too busy working on his own dream."

"What's he studying?"

"I'm not exactly sure, but it's some specialized field in mathematics. I can't understand it even enough to explain it. He's hoping to win the Fields Medal someday."

"The Fields Medal?" Michizuka asked, a little incredulous. Then he backpedaled—he did not want to be dismissive of my boyfriend. "It's that math award they give out only once every four years, right? The 'Nobel Prize of Mathematics'?"

"That's the one. But I know he can do it. It's been his dream since he was a child."

"Seriously? He must have been one unusual kid."

"Obviously, it wasn't some specific goal for him back then. I mean, he didn't even know there was no Nobel Prize of Mathematics until the summer of his third year in middle school, and he only found out because his teacher told him. His first dream was actually to become a soccer player, but he had to give up on that dream early on."

"Why's that?"

"When he was in second grade, he lost his right leg in a bus accident. The same accident in which my mother died."

Michizuka stopped sipping his coffee, shocked.

"But he found a new dream," I continued. "The world he was handed was a raw deal, but he overcame his handicap and made it all the way into grad school. And starting next year, he'll be continuing his research as a professor working at the same university. That's why there's no chance that work will ever come between us. I mean, I don't even understand calculus."

"Wow. Honestly, that's impressive." Michizuka gazed admiringly into empty space, as if my boyfriend were sitting right there.

"So, now you know. He's not the kind of clingy, needy boy who's going to freak out about me starting a company with another guy. And that our relationship's made of the same sturdy stuff."

"Okay, I get it. Geez!" Michizuka teased, grinning.

We left the restaurant and exchanged a firm handshake in the lobby of the hotel. It would be just the two of us in the beginning. But how would things look a year from now? Or even three years? No, everything would work out fine. With the top two salespeople of Inspire working together, there was nothing we couldn't accomplish.

"Well, I'm going to go now. I can't wait to tell my boyfriend about the school."

"He'll be happy to hear it, I bet."

"Of course. Knowing him, he's going to do whatever he can to support me. He might be just a little surprised though."

"Well, yeah, I mean deciding to do something like that on your last day at Inspire? And on top of that, already hiring somebody? His eyes are going to pop right out of their sockets."

"Wait till I tell him we already have a company name. That'll make his jaw fall right off."

"What?" he asked, surprised. "So we're actually going with that?"

I looked away from Michizuka and up at the sky. It was speckled with hundreds of stars, like little holes in a dark fabric through which warm light poured in.

I thought about how, like myself, those stars managed to be stars because they didn't blend in with the space around them. *Thank you, Mr. Watanabe,* I thought. *Once again, you helped save me from myself.*

I cupped my mouth with my hands and shouted at the brightest star in the sky.

"Tearing down the starting stretch, iiiit's Roadstaaar!"

The Tale of the Ring Finger

Kanayo is the sweetest little angel, running around merrily all day without a care in the world. She has a bit of temper sometimes, but deep down, she's a really nice girl.

Me? Oh, I'm Ring. Kanayo's ring finger. Since Kanayo is six years old, I guess that makes me six years old, too!

Now, let me introduce you to the rest of the family.

Three fingers to my right is my dad—Kanayo's thumb. He's the strongest, biggest dad in the world!

To his left is my mom, Kanayo's index finger. She's very elegant—the index finger next door on Kanayo's right hand is always saying so.

Between me and my mom is my big brother, the middle finger. He's very tall. I hope that one day, I'll be as tall as he is.

To my left is my little sister, Kanayo's pinkie. She's scrappy—a little bit of a tomboy.

Now, there's something that's been worrying me. I know what you're thinking—but just because I'm little doesn't mean I don't have worries!

Since starting elementary school, Kanayo's been learning to play the piano. But her technique hasn't been improving, which makes her *really* angry. What's been bothering me is... it's all my fault.

I'm always the one messing up when she plays. Like, sometimes I press the key down too late. Or I flub and play a note that my sister was supposed to play.

The middle finger next door was so annoyed with me. "Why are you so slow, Ring?" he asked me just yesterday. "Why can't you be nimble like the rest of us?"

Luckily, my dad defended me, telling him that we were both on Kanayo's hands, and that we needed to get along. But that doesn't change the fact that middle finger was right. I *am* a slow-poke. I must have looked really blue, because my dad then said to me, "Chin up, Ring. One day you're going to be appreciated for all your hard work."

Six years later, Kanayo was in a piano competition. By now she was twelve years old. Kanayo looked so pretty—she was wearing a dress she bought just for the occasion. As she climbed onto the stage, I could tell she was nervous. I could feel her heart racing, even all the way down here. There were so many people in the audience—more than I'd seen in my entire life!

She sat in front of the piano and readied herself to play.

I was so nervous—and it wasn't just me. Even my dad and that stupid middle finger next door were holding their breath in anticipation.

And then, she started to play.

Everyone was playing perfectly, as we were meant to, dancing over the keys. It was the best we had ever played. Until I did it again.

I'd been doing so well in recent lessons, but now, when it counted the most, I hit the wrong key.

The crowd began to murmur. I could feel the stares of the people sitting in the audience, embarrassed for Kanayo. It was painful.

I don't remember what happened after that. And if I couldn't even remember, then I must not have been hitting the right notes.

At the end, the crowd burst into applause, and Kanayo made a light bow. But as soon as she returned to the dressing room, she ran into her mother's arms and began sobbing.

She said she never wanted to play the piano again.

Then she glared at me and called me "useless."

She was right. I was useless.

She loved playing the piano and, because of me, she gave it up.

I figured I should run away. She wouldn't mind if I wasn't there—in fact, she'd probably be happy to be rid of me.

But, that evening, my mom said to me:

"There are no useless fingers in the world, Ring."

I wasn't easily consoled, but I took her words to heart and didn't run away. From that day on, all I could do was work hard and try to improve in the things that came so difficult to me.

But I continued my streak of uselessness. I kept making the same clumsy mistakes over and over.

I was so different from the other fingers that it made me cry.

It made me so angry that I couldn't be agile like the other fingers, and that just led to more crying.

It seemed like crying was the only thing I was good at.

Many years passed.

One night, Kanayo went out on a date with her boyfriend. They looked happy, as usual, but suddenly the mood changed. Her boyfriend was acting so stiff and nervous. Then I noticed that Kanayo seemed anxious, too.

Her boyfriend asked her a question, and Kanayo replied.

"Yes."

Then her boyfriend lifted up her left hand—the hand with me and my family—and did something very unexpected.

He put a sparkling ring on me.

What was this ring with this huge jewel on top of it? It was so bright that I had to cover my eyes! Why was he putting this thing on me? Was it punishment? Was this another cruel reminder about how useless I was?

"Ring, dear," my mother said to me. "That's called an engagement ring. Kanayo was just proposed to by her boyfriend."

"Proposed? What does that mean, mom?"

"It's when a man asks a woman for her hand in marriage."

Marriage?! That's something Kanayo's dreamed about for a very long time. "But mom… if he put the ring on me, that means…?"

"Yes, dear. She accepted his proposal. Which means they're going to get married. An engagement ring is very important—very special. It is irreplaceable, and you will be in charge of it as long as you both live."

"But why did Kanayo allow such an important object to be placed on me? Why did she choose me when I'm so useless?"

"That's because Kanayo really loves you, dear. Don't you remember what I told you a long time ago?"

There are no useless fingers in the world, Ring.

I was glad—so glad that I had never stopped working hard.

No matter how hard I tried, I had always managed to get in Kanayo's way.

But Kanayo had still taken care of me in spite of all that.

She loved me for who I was.

I was glad I never gave up.

While thinking about this, something very strange happened. I was genuinely happy, but for some reason, I started crying. This was so confusing. I was used to crying by then—I'd probably cried hundreds of times. But it was usually because I was sad, or because I was angry at myself.

"Ring," my father explained with a smile, "Those kinds of tears are only achieved by those who've had to work very hard in their lives. Only those who've worked tirelessly are allowed to cry when they're happy."

Kanayo was also crying as she leaned into her boyfriend, holding him tightly.

*   *   *

Dai tiptoed into the room, a postcard in his hand. Ayu, sitting on the floor, closed the picture book she was reading. Yuko was asleep beside her.

"Hey, you," Ayu said, turning to her husband.

"She's already fallen asleep?"

"Yeah. I think this book is a tad advanced for her."

"Probably," Dai said. "Geez. Someday, that day's going to come for her, and then she'll be leaving us for a new life."

"Oh, god, don't tell me you're already worrying about losing her to her future husband!"

Dai looked so earnestly distressed that Ayu had to hold back from laughing. Dai, feeling embarrassed, changed the subject.

"She's going to be a big sister soon," he whispered, kneeling down and pressing his ear to her stomach.

"What're you doing?"

"Trying to hear what Takuya's saying."

"And at what point did we decide on Takuya, mister? Besides, we still don't know if it's a boy or girl yet."

Dai laughed.

"What's that postcard?" Ayu asked.

"It's from America."

"Really? From who?"

"A former student. Remember that girl from… I guess it would be four years ago? Who was putting ready-made meals into her lunchbox during summer school?"

Ayu narrowed her eyes, filing through her memory. Then they widened. "Oh, that girl! What was her name again?"

"Lisa Hoshino."

"Right. The girl who wanted to go to America for college."

"Ever since her first year in middle school."

"So I guess Lisa's dream came true," Ayu replied with admiration.

"Yup. She's already on summer vacation. Do you know what the coolest thing is, though?"

"What's that?"

"She's already decided what she wants to do after graduation: come home and open an English-language school."

"Wow. Well, knowing her, she's probably not going to give herself a moment's rest until it happens."

Dai looked at Lisa—now grown up—smiling back at him from the postcard.

Remember, Lisa. You have to start by finding the mountain. Once you've done that, you can make your way to the foot of that mountain. If you were to walk to Mt. Fuji from Tokyo, even if you didn't know the way, you'd be able to find it, because the top is always visible. If you can't find the mountain, it means you're looking for a dream that doesn't really exist in your world.

Once you get to the foot of the mountain, the rest is easy. All you need to do is change your angle one degree per day. As long as you keep walking, you'll eventually make it to the top.

Knowing the circumstances in which you grew up, the biggest fear that'll devour you is the fear of being poor. You might decide to change your course, put on a sharp suit and work for a major corporation. If that happens, don't worry; you haven't fallen off your path yet.

There's no such thing as a straight line to the top, Lisa. A mountain path curves along the ridges of the mountain. It does that to make it easier for you to climb the entire mountain.

There are two types of people, Lisa. There are those who dismiss what may seem like a pointless experience, calling it a waste. Then there are those who can turn it into the food that sustains them. You're one of the latter, Lisa. That's why I believe in you, and believe that one day, your dream will come true.

If you ever feel lost, Lisa, look at that business card I gave you. Look at it and remind yourself of who you are: the black circle.

"What are you thinking about, my love?"

"Hm? Oh, nothing…" and then, "do you remember our little entomologist? I had a pretty interesting conversation with him today. He came in for extra credit, and, at one point, he told me he wanted to win the Nobel Prize in Mathematics. So I told him about the Fields Medal."

"Aww. He's so good at math, you sometimes forget he's only in his third year of middle school. Well, it's a good thing you didn't tell him that there's no Nobel Prize in Math and just leave it at that. Now he still has something to work for. Funny, huh? How we both had him as a student?"

"Yeah." Dai looked down at Yuko for a moment before continuing. "I have this feeling he might actually win it, you know."

"The Fields Medal?"

"Yeah. It's almost like it's sitting there, waiting for him. Like it's just meant to be."

Ayu nodded.

"All right, let's go to bed, Ayu. You've got a big day tomorrow."

"Yeah." Ayu wondered how the bride would look at the reception.

Dai laid out two futons, one on each side of Yuko. Ayu laid down first. "She says she's going to quit her job after tomorrow," Ayu said as Dai was about to turn off the light.

"So she's not going to work anymore?"

"No. She just won the new writers award in the Satsuki

Grand Prize for Japanese Literature. She's finally going to quit her job at the bar so she can focus on her writing."

"Wow. That's impressive."

"Well, even though she didn't end up teaching, I'm glad she was my student teacher." Ayu situated herself. "Anyway, she told me that her fiancé is also going to quit his job at the bank to start his own company. She said he always saw himself leaving once he'd saved enough money and gained enough experience, and, apparently, he decided now was the right time. So it'll be a triple celebration—for the wedding, the writing prize, *and* the new company."

"Sounds like a full party," Dai sighed happily. He switched off the light and lay down on his futon, facing her.

"You are so going to cry tomorrow."

"I am *not* going to cry."

"You cried at our wedding."

"I did not."

"You know you did."

"Shut up, Dai."

Then silence enveloped the three—or four, including the future addition to the family. And, soon, they were carried by their dreams into a world of elegant imagination, where they would stay until the warm light of day brought them back to reality.

Then, they would bask in the brightness of the summer sun,

spread equally among those who walked below it.

Afterword

A common perception is that fiction writers create stories out of thin air. That may be the case for some stories, but there are also stories that come together naturally when forgotten incidents from the past begin to intertwine within the subconscious.

When I was in my first year of middle school, I played on the school volleyball team. One of my teammates, who was two years ahead of me, had a bad right leg—the result of a traffic accident from two years before. He still came to practice everyday, arriving at the court earlier than everyone else and dashing back and forth during practice to pick up stray balls without complaint. During matches, he cheered for the team more enthusiastically than anyone else. I really looked up to him.

That fall, we had a sports day. One of the events was a 150-meter (150 yd.) dash, with heats held in order of school year. Having finished my heat, I sat down to watch the second- and third-year students race. To my surprise, I saw my friend standing at the starting line.

As soon as the pistol went off, it was clear that my friend was going to come in last. He wasn't even running—he was dragging his right leg and practically walking towards the finish line. Suddenly, there was a change in the mood. The students who had been sitting down all stood up and joined the parents who had come to watch in cheering for my friend. Even the school PA system, which had been playing music the entire time, was now broadcasting the cheers of a teacher who had taken control of the microphone.

It was all a wonderful sight, but something about it bothered me. In any race, someone was always bound to come in last. So why was everybody cheering on my friend when they hadn't offered the same courtesy to the other students who had come in last? After all, my friend had the option of staying out of the race due to his leg.

I now understand that my friend had decided to compete in the race because he did not want to be treated differently from the other students. I can also imagine what was going through his head as he ran around the track. But as a 12-year-old, I was unable to put a finger on what bothered me.

Years later, I was in high school, working my first part-time job catching stag beetles by the Fuji River that ran along the foot of Mt. Fuji, and selling them to insect shops located in department stores. It was a difficult job to get the hang of and, in the beginning, I made some pretty careless mistakes—a major one being causing the beetles to lose a leg by being overly aggressive when pulling them from the branch when they refused to let go of the tree they were clinging onto. The shops would put these beetles into boxes labeled "Chip" (meaning "Defected") and sell them for almost nothing. In the end, I decided not to sell a single "chipped" beetle to the stores. I felt that, as the person who had caused them to be defective, it was my duty to raise them.

Several years passed and I was a college student. During

summer vacation one year, I experienced the biggest shock of my life. I was working as a waiter in a restaurant when I noticed that one customer made a dull metallic sound every time he walked. I must have been looking at him strangely because he gestured for me to come over. When I did, he rolled up his right trouser leg... and I witnessed my first-ever prosthetic leg. I had always assumed that prosthetics were shiny and silver, so I was shocked to see the color of this prosthetic match the color of the man's skin.

It was at that moment that it all made sense. The discomfort I had felt at the crowd cheering on my friend during that race in middle school; the stag beetles I had caused to become defective while hunting for them in high school; and the metallic clang created by this prosthetic leg. These disparate experiences came together like pieces of a puzzle and became a single vision. It was like watching a movie unfold.

After I finished work that day, I went home and wrote a short story in two hours. That became my first work: "The Boy and the Beetles." It was 1984, and I was only 18 years old.

Twenty-three years later, in 2007, *Every Little Thing* was published in Japan. It was not that I had taken that long to complete the book—but after graduating college, I spent some time working as an in-house programmer, followed by a stint as a freelance IT writer. It was not until 2004 that I began seriously considering becoming a novelist. The first work of fiction I completed is the book you are reading right now.

Things did not go as I had planned. I submitted my work

to dozens of publishers, but they all rejected my manuscript. It didn't help that it took a very long time to hear back from them. The waiting game really killed me.

The worst part was that instead of focusing on the quality of the work, most of the rejection letters stressed the same thing: that because I was an unknown writer, they didn't feel my work would sell well. This was my first work—of course I would be unknown. If that was the only criteria for getting published, I thought, I might never launch my career as a novelist. I felt like a worm that had foolishly come out of the ground in the middle of summer and ended up frying on the asphalt.

Finally, I experienced the worst humiliation of my life. An editor of a certain publisher called to ask if I could come over and bring my work with me. He told me he didn't want to waste my time, and would read my manuscript then and there to give me his assessment. I was so thrilled to finally encounter an editor who understood the torture of waiting; this man, I was sure, would accept my manuscript. I even called my worried parents to tell them my work would finally be published.

I headed for the publisher, my heart skipping. He was right. He didn't end up wasting any of my time. Two minutes into reading the manuscript, the editor returned it to me and said, "I'm sorry, but I really have no desire to read any further."

I thanked him for taking the time to read my manuscript and apologized for having wasted his time. Then I left the building and immediately dashed into a nearby alleyway. And I cried. After three years of trying unsuccessfully to sell *Every Little Thing*, I cried for the first time. For a full ten minutes, I cried out loud like a miserable child. Whenever I remember that moment, I am still surprised at how many tears a single man can shed.

Flash forward a few years, and *Every Little Thing*, after having been rejected by dozens of editors, is now a Japanese bestseller, has been translated into Korean and Chinese, and has now been published in the biggest market of the world, America. It's really funny how life works. I feel like I've been transposed into the world of *Every Little Thing*.

Looking back on those years, the only thing I can say for certain is that although effort may not lead to success, it will lead to personal growth. That is what makes effort so important in my eyes.

Very few novelists in Japan bother to write an afterword like this, or to thank the various people who were involved in crafting the work. But this being my first book published in America, I've decided to ignore what's typical in Japan and write a proper afterword, acknowledgments included.

I would like to extend my sincere gratitude to each and every person who helped me publish and promote my book. Special thanks goes out to the Soli Consultants team, who included: Zal Heiwa Sethna, who translated the book; Cyrus Nozomu Sethna, who directed the audio reading for "The Boy and the Beetles" and also played the narrator and the shopkeeper; Shannon Latimer, who polished the translation; and Rumiko Varnes, who played the boy in the reading. Special thanks also goes to the Babel Corporation team, namely company president Tomoki Hotta, project coordinator Junko Rodriguez, layout designer Sota Torigoe, and editor Kanae Ervin.

And finally, I'd like to thank you, the reader. Words can't express how grateful I am for your picking up this book.

Here in Japan, I've just published a sequel to *Every Little Thing*. Many of you may have noticed that "The Tale of the Ring Finger" does not feature Tomoro and Naomi from "After the Prom" at all. There was a reason for this—the sequel will begin with the two starting their college lives.

If this book has whetted your appetite for this sequel, there is nothing more that I could ask of you.

Ash Omurah